SUNFLOWERS AND SABOTAGE

PORT DANBY COZY MYSTERY #10

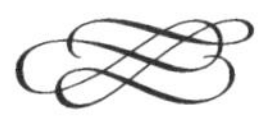

LONDON LOVETT

Sunflowers and Sabotage

ISBN: 9781072921769

Imprint: Independently published

CHAPTER 1

Bear turned his big head toward the sound of Briggs' whistle and came bounding back toward us, his oversized paws splashing through the frothy shoreline and his elephant style ears flapping in every direction.

The sight of Bear loping always gave me a good laugh. "I believe your dog has mastered the art of galumphing."

Briggs nodded. "And as a parent, I can say I'm just proud that he's turned galumphing into an art. Is this a good spot?"

I turned around and inspected our chosen patch of sand. "Let's see—close enough to the water to feel its cooling spray, yet not so close that we'll have to jump up and grab all of our stuff out of the way of a rogue wave." I squinted up to the sky. It was early evening, but there were still a good two hours of sun. "Sun is at just the right angle to keep us toasty without shining directly in our eyes." I smiled at him. There was no finer sight than Detective James Briggs with ocean breeze swept hair and a scruffy five o'clock shadow. "It's perfect."

"Can't help but love a girl who methodically reasons out where to sit on the beach." Briggs set down the ice chest and pulled the blanket out from under his arm. We struggled against the aforementioned ocean breeze for a few minutes to get the blanket under control. The blue cotton throw finally surrendered its fight and floated serenely down on the sand just in time for Bear to land right in the center for a good salt water shake. Briggs and I simultaneously ducked away from the sea water spray coming off of the dog's fur.

"Well done, you big oaf," Briggs said. "I take back my proud parent comment." He nudged the dog to move to a corner of the blanket. "It's a little wet and sandy now. Should we shake it off?"

I circled my arm around. "I don't think we can avoid the sand. Besides, it gives our beach dinner a little ambience."

Three sandpipers were making their way along the water's edge engaged in a serious search for tiny crabs. Bear hopped up to his big paws and trotted down to the water to see if he could join them. They weren't too keen on the idea. The three birds raced on skinny legs down the sand. Bear trotted blithely behind them.

I hopped up on my knees and opened the ice chest. "Now remember, you promised to keep an open mind about these veggie sandwiches," I reminded him as I reached into the chest to pull out the food. "I stuffed two whole wheat rolls with a host of fresh goodies, all nutritious and healthy and vitamin-y that will make you grow tall and put hair on your—" I stopped short of finishing my commercial, blushing at the possible ways to end it.

My cheeks still warm, I handed Briggs his sandwich without looking him straight in the eye. However, I could feel his dark eyes on me.

"I'm waiting for you to finish," he teased. "I'm going to grow tall and there will be hair on my—?"

"Oh, stop it." I sat down. "Besides, that shouldn't be the most interesting part of my claim. After all, when was the last time you grew taller?"

He unwrapped his sandwich. "Hmm, I'd say just after my eighteenth birthday. I remember because I got a new pair of Levis and a month later my socks were showing."

I laughed. "Got to love a man who takes a completely rhetorical question and provides a detailed answer."

He reached for my hand and yanked me forward. I nearly fell into his lap. He kissed me. "If that's what it takes to win your love, then fire away with the rhetoricals."

I kissed him back and sat down on the blanket. Bear's attention had been stolen by the addition of another dog to the sandpiper chasing fun. His new friend seemed to be an eclectic mix of golden retriever and dachshund. Everything about the top half of the dog said normal everyday retriever, but the bottom half was completely dachshund.

Briggs caught the inconsistency too. "That dog looks as if he's a golden retriever standing in a hole. Where's the rest of him?"

Bear swung around and gave the dog a friendly pat with his big paw. The two played gently with each other, seemingly no longer interested in harassing sandpipers.

"See, Bear is such a good guy," I said. "No judgment or short jokes, just hello new friend, let's play."

The dog's owner, or *person* to be more politically correct since most of us tended to be owned by our pets more than the other way around, was a tall, lanky forty something woman wearing a purple sundress. She had set her chair and towel down about fifty feet from our evening picnic. A very imperious looking and beautiful gray standard poodle sat obediently next to her on its own towel. The poodle stared out at the two goofballs having fun down at the shoreline. I wondered if the poodle was watching them with derision, (silly, sloppy mutts giving the rest of us a bad name) or with envy, (wish I could just throw caution to the wind and roll in the wet sand).

I took a bite of my veggie sandwich. The layer of hummus and avocado was flavorful and creamy beneath the piles of cucumber, sliced radish and spinach. "Hmm, this is even better than I thought." I looked at Briggs who was on his second bite. "Well, don't keep me in suspense."

He nodded as he swallowed. "Very tasty. So what has us eating rabbit food? Is Elsie still on a health food kick? Rather hypocritical considering what the woman has done for the community's collective sugar and fat consumption."

"First of all, Elsie doesn't go on a *kick* . . . ever. A kick implies some sort of impetuous, flighty, sure-to fail spur of the moment idea. Elsie Norris throws her entire mind, body and soul into her plans, and this one was borne mostly from her brother's last physical. Les had both high blood sugar and cholesterol."

"I rest my case about my earlier comment." Briggs picked up a slice of fallen radish and tossed it onto the sand. A piece of cucumber slipped out next. "Lots of things trying to escape this sandwich. I think you need to slather mayonnaise on the bread to keep the veggies in line."

"Any condiment that requires slathering shouldn't be anywhere near a healthy sandwich. As I was saying, this isn't just a *kick* for Elsie. She is determined to change Les's unhealthy habits. She's even going to add some vegan choices at her bakery."

Briggs shook his head. "Those two words—vegan and bakery—should never be used in the same sentence. However, I am truly enjoying this sandwich." He took another big bite.

Bear seemed to have noticed that we were eating. He left his new friend slightly bewildered and sad as Bear galloped back to our blanket. The short retriever decided to follow.

"Looks like we're going to be overrun by sandy, wet dogs," Briggs said.

I hopped up on my knees. "I brought some of Elsie's peanut butter dog treats." Elsie, the genius town baker, had come up with the clever plan to sell dog treats from her bakery. They were a hit. Rarely did a dog loving customer leave without purchasing a treat for Fido too. I pulled out two bone shaped peanut butter dog cookies.

The other dog's owner, the woman in the purple dress, hopped up from her towel. "Trigger, don't bother those people," she called. "Come here right now."

I waved. "It's all right. Can he have a peanut butter dog treat?" I called back.

She smiled and waved in return. "Sure, thank you." She said something to the poodle. The impeccably groomed dog sat down on its haunches, then the woman headed our direction.

"Now you've done it," Briggs muttered. "Our romantic picnic has turned into a dog party."

I handed Bear and Trigger the treats. They each found a corner of the blanket to sit and enjoy the cookies. The woman struggled to keep her naturally curly brown hair in check as she hiked across the sand. I could sympathize completely. I'd given up on trying to tame my natural curls just a month after moving to Port Danby.

"I'm so sorry about my dog. He knows better than to run onto someone else's beach blanket," the woman said as she reached us.

"Not at all," I said. "Bear is happy to have a new friend."

She laughed. "They did seem to hit it off right away. Unfortunately, his usual friend, Pebbles"—she motioned back to her poodle —"has been groomed for a show, so she's not allowed to play."

"What a coincidence, I'm making sunflower arrangements for a dog show. I own Pink's Flowers."

"What fun. I'd love to be surrounded by flowers all day," she said.

"Is she entered in the Chesterton Dog Show?" Briggs asked. "I saw them setting up for the event when I drove past the park today."

"Yes, it's a big deal. We're really hoping we take the grand champion ribbon this year," she said.

"Pebbles is a stunning dog," I said. "Good luck."

"Thank you. We've been working hard for this show. Pebbles is well-trained. Unfortunately, I've been neglectful about Trigger's training."

Right then, Bear, now finished with his treat, hopped up and pounced on Briggs. "As you can see," he said as he scrubbed Bear's head, "we've been sort of neglectful on that front too."

The woman laughed. "No wonder they get along so well." She pulled a business card out from her pocket. "I would love to make up for the mess my dog made on your blanket." She handed me the card. "I'm Ellen Joyner. I have an online store with an entire line of dog grooming products. My Lavender Pooch is my most popular shampoo. It can make your dog smell like a field of lavender. At least, in between swims in the ocean and rolls in the sand. Just type Pebbles in the coupon code and you'll get a twenty percent discount."

"Thank you." I handed the card to Briggs. "And again, good luck at the show."

"Come on, Trigger, you've bothered these people long enough." Trigger was hesitant to leave Bear, but a long withering look from his owner pushed him to his feet and he trotted after her.

Bear flopped down for a nap. "I don't know if Bear is the lavender type," Briggs said. "He's more a leather or musk or—what's another manly scent?"

"Testosterone?" I suggested.

Briggs smiled at me. "Even you and your super nose can't smell testosterone."

"Don't need to. It's more of an attitude than a fragrance. And it's not always a pleasant one either."

"I suppose you're right on all accounts." He maneuvered himself so that he was sitting right next to me with a perfect view of the water. "Nothing like a long summer evening with my favorite person and my big, wet dog."

I rested my head against his shoulder. "Yep. I've been complaining about the heat too much. Truth is, I'm going to miss these warm August nights."

CHAPTER 2

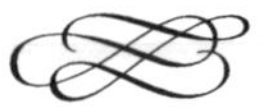

I finished tying the paw print ribbon around the last vase. I leaned back to get a good look at the arrangements. Bright yellow and orange sunflowers were nestled between stalks of blue delphinium and dotted with green button poms. "Your suggestion to add in the green button poms was brilliant," I told my shop assistant, Ryder, as he put finishing touches on each arrangement.

"Thanks. I thought between the royal blue of the delphinium and fiery mix of sunflowers, a spot of green here and there helped bring it back to earth."

I nodded. "Well put. Hopefully, I can get these arrangements to the dog show without any catastrophes. These tall bouquets are always less balanced." I walked to end of the work island and picked up the broom. "James and I actually saw one of the dog show contestants at the beach last night. She was quite the stunner with her poodle pompoms. Her owner had another dog with her, an odd looking but sweet retriever dachshund mix."

Ryder laughed. "Those wiener dogs sure do get around. My

neighbor has a collie mixed with a doxie, and it looks as if someone cut it off at the knees."

"Guess those short, squat genes are dominant." The door opened as I said it.

Les sighed loudly. "Are you guys talking about me? I heard someone say short and squat." Les was carrying a bowl that seemed to be brimming with a host of grilled vegetables. "Would you look at this, Ryder? Elsie calls this lunch."

Ryder and I walked over to peer into his bowl. Grilled zucchini, onions and sweet potatoes were nestled deliciously on a bed of quinoa. My nose picked up paprika and a dash of garlic salt.

"Hey, bro, that looks like a pretty sweet lunch to me," Ryder said. "And your heart will thank you afterwards."

"My heart might thank me but my stomach is saying 'have you lost your mind?'" Les sat on a stool at the work island. "Maybe if I eat amongst friends, it will be more fulfilling. Nice sunflowers, by the way."

"Thanks, they're for the dog show." I started sweeping the floor.

Kingston smelled the hot food and dropped right down from his perch to march purposefully across the floor

"Watch out, Les, looks like King is making a beeline for your veggie lunch," Ryder warned.

Kingston reached the stools and shook his shiny black feathers once before hopping up onto the counter. His black eyes zeroed in on Les's bowl.

Les didn't hesitate to drop a piece of zucchini on the counter for the bird. "I think I've just figured out a way to make these healthy lunches disappear and all without the torture of eating them myself."

Kingston picked up the slice of limp zucchini, tossed it around a few times and then dropped it back on the counter.

"Good try, Les," I laughed. "Unfortunately, Kingston feels the same way about cooked veggies as you. Looks like you'll have to eat the bowl all by yourself."

Les put down his fork. "I think the woman is trying to kill me with all this fiber. I'm going to blow up like a helium balloon and float away if I eat much more of this roughage. And then there's the philosophical conundrum," Les added.

Ryder and I looked at each other and shrugged.

"What philosophical conundrum is that?" Ryder asked.

Les swiveled on the stool to look at him. "Is life really worth living if it's void of cheeseburgers and malts? I mean, she's trying to save my life, but how long should I be expected to stay on earth without the occasional cheeseburger?"

I leaned the broom against the counter and walked over to the side where Les was sitting. I could see the entire diet idea was really upsetting him. Les was always jovial and easy going, but the bowl of vegetables in front of him seemed to be sucking the life right out of him. I sat on the stool. Kingston shifted from foot to foot, like an anxious kid, waiting and hoping that something much better would be coming out of the bowl than zucchini.

"Les, Elsie isn't doing this to torture you. She loves you and she wants you to be healthy. I know she can be somewhat controlling—"

Les's laugh nearly shook him off the stool. "If that isn't the understatement of the year."

"All right. Elsie likes to control things, but that's one of the things we love about her. Otherwise, she wouldn't be Elsie. Why don't you make a compromise with her? Tell her you'll eat healthy, the foods she wants you to eat, for five days but then on the weekend you get to splurge. She might go for that, and I think you'll still see a big improvement on your cholesterol."

Les picked up the fork and moved the veggies around in the quinoa as if they might disappear if he stirred them enough. "That sounds more like a plan I could stick to. If I knew I could sit down with the guys and have a beer and nachos on Saturday night, I might be able to eat this strange stuff in between."

I laughed. "It's really not all that strange. Those are all vegetables that you can find sitting right in the produce section of the store."

He turned to me and blinked under his fluffy white mop of hair. "Exactly where is this mythical produce section?"

I nudged his shoulder. "You are worse than a kid when it comes to vegetables. Ask Elsie about the compromise. I think she'll agree." I hopped off the stool.

"I'll try but I think you're talking about the wrong Elsie. The one I know isn't too keen on compromise." He dug his fork into the bowl and plucked out a piece of sweet potato.

I nodded at Ryder. "One more fire extinguished. Just point out my next problem to solve."

Right then, Lola walked into the shop. She didn't take two steps before she sighed heavily. "What do you suppose the odds are that I could be abducted by aliens sometime in the next few hours before my parents get home?"

Ryder waved at her with a flourish and bowed his head at me. "Solver, I present you with your next problem."

"I don't have a problem," Lola insisted as she walked toward the stools. "I have *two* problems. One is named Dad and one is Mom. Or John and Cynthia as they are known in their social circles." She hopped on the stool next to Les. It seemed my shop stools, ones intended for customers to use while they browsed through catalogs, were moonlighting as therapist couches today.

"Lo-lo," Ryder said in the sing song tone he always used when he brought out the nickname. He walked over, picked up one of the unused sunflowers and handed it to her. "You don't have to worry about your parents' visit. I, on the other hand, am silently freaking out about it. You just can't see it through my steady as steel veneer."

I joined the group at the work island, deciding there was far too much going on to ignore. "Why are you freaking out?" I asked. "Why is everyone freaking out? Les, stop procrastinating and eat your vegetables. Lola, stop worrying about your parents' visit. My parents visited a few months back and I survived unscathed." I held out my arms to prove my point but then was suddenly reminded about a rather public and vivid conversation, or, more accurately, argument with my mom about me spending far too much budget on decorative vases and expensive ribbons. It had left me feeling like a chastised little kid, and my mom and I didn't speak for an entire day. Then I came home to a batch of her chocolate chip cookies and I forgave her. (Making the little kid analogy even more accurate.) "Well, mostly unscathed," I added, knowing that both Lola and Ryder and even Elsie had witnessed the decorative vase argument firsthand.

"Anyhow, I'm sure your mom is nothing compared to mine," I continued.

A short, derisive laugh shot from Lola's mouth. "You've only met my mom briefly on that time they stopped in Port Danby on their way to South America. She was too jetlagged after their flight from Spain to be her normal self. This trip, she'll have to time to peel away the jet lag and show her true self. And, I can tell you that Cynthia Button could give your Peggy Pinkerton a run for her money. In fact, I'll bet everyone here that her first comment will be something about my appearance. She'll turn her lip up at my Stone Temple Pilots' t-shirt. Or, she'll ask, 'was your hair always so curly' or 'was it always so red'? And she'll ask it with all seriousness as if she didn't ever notice that her one and only daughter had curly red hair."

"Last time my mom visited, she asked me if I'd broken my nose because she had never noticed this little bump on the bridge." I rubbed my nose to point out the flaw, although it probably didn't need highlighting. "So there, I can take your mom's passively judgmental comments and raise you a broken nose. And, no, by the way, it was never broken, and the bump was always there."

"Maybe it's from all that super sniffing you do," Les said with a laugh. He saw his comment fell flat. "I don't think this conversation is making these vegetables go down any smoother, so I'll be on my way." He hopped off the stool and winked my direction. "You have a cute nose. I'm going to see if your idea works. Maybe Elsie will give me some slack."

"Good plan," I winked back.

He hurried out the door with his bowl of mostly uneaten food.

Ryder picked up the broom to finish where I left off. "All I know is, this is the first time I'm going to meet your parents. I'm worried they won't like me."

"What's not to like?" I asked. "You are every parent's dream boyfriend."

"I'm not rich," he said. "I know that's on every parent's list for a dream boyfriend."

Lola looked at me. "He's right. Rich is number two on the list right under must have important connections in the antique world."

"Great, I've already lost on one and two," Ryder complained.

Lola hopped off the stool and walked around to his side. "You forget, I don't care what they think of you. Besides, Lacey is right. What's not to like? You are perfect in every way." She hopped up on her toes and kissed him. "Except the whole rich and antique thing," she added, unhelpfully.

"All right, I think all of us have had enough of a pity party," I said. "I've got to get the sunflower arrangements out to Chesterton Park for the dog show."

"I'll come with you to help," Lola said. "I could use a break from the shop. I've been cleaning and dusting and shining all day just to make sure the place sparkles for the visit. Not that it will matter because my mom will still find something to criticize."

I handed Lola two of the arrangements. "Hey, pity party ended, remember? Here you go. I'm happy to have the help."

CHAPTER 3

Chesterton Park was an impressive expanse of green space that was dotted with lush sycamores and walnut trees for shade. A children's playground, complete with tall twisting slide and a climbing wall, took up one corner of the park, while the rest of the space was covered with sports fields and walking paths. The Chesterton Dog Show occupied most of the free space. Competitors had set up portable kennels and dog runs along the paths. The more serious competitors had arrived in custom coaches, namely small motorhomes that were decorated with the names of the contestants. Some of the competitors had set up elaborate campsites equipped with mini refrigerators, chairs and grooming stations. Vendors were setting up pop-up kiosks and tables to display their products. A trailer set up near the vendors boasted that it was a traveling beauty salon for last minute touch-ups. The words The Foxy Dog Salon were painted on the side in fancy orange lettering. Across the field, a show stage had been set up on the baseball diamond. Several men were testing the sound system.

Lola and I carried the arrangements across the field to the stage. "I need to find a woman named Terry. She's in charge of decorating the stage. I only met her once. She has short white hair and bright blue glasses."

Lola leaned side to side to see where she was going past the sunflowers. "These bouquets make it a little hard to scout out a lady with white hair and blue glasses. Maybe we should put them down somewhere first."

"Good idea. Let's place them on the stage. I think that's where they are going anyhow. Then we can look for Terry."

With the arrangements tucked away safely on the stage, Lola and I were free to meander along the paths and admire all the beautiful dogs. One Bichon Frise was so fluffy and white like a cloud, he looked as if he had been plucked from the summer sky. His owner was sitting in a chair near the portable pen knitting what appeared to be a tiny sweater. A pair of Silky Terriers yapped away in the next pen. Each was wearing a colorful bow. Their coats were so shiny I could almost see myself .

Lola laughed. "Maybe I should bring Late Bloomer out here. Do you think they have a stinkiest dog category?"

"Oh, don't make fun of Bloomer. He's one of the finest dogs I know," I said.

"I agree. But since I work with him all day and then sleep in the same bed with him at night, I think I have a right to bring up his stinks. And they are numerous and occasionally make your eyes water."

"Speaking of making my eyes water—" I partially covered my nose to stop the onslaught of fragrances drifting toward us from every direction. My hand wasn't helping. I found myself, or, more accurately, my super sensitive nose, becoming more and more overwhelmed by the strong fragrances in the air. I stopped to stifle a sneeze. "Oh wow, I feel like I just walked into the perfume department in the store." A quick set of sneezes followed.

"Here you go," the nice woman knitting the dog sweater chirruped from behind. She held out a tissue.

I walked back to her. "Thank you very much. There are a lot of scents floating around. I'm smelling a lot of lavender."

The woman nodded. "You've got a good nose."

Lola snorted. "There's an understatement if I've ever heard one," she muttered under her breath.

"Most of us use Ellen Joyner's Lavender Pooch shampoo for shows," the woman continued. "It leaves Danny's coat feeling like silk." She leaned down to run her fingertips over her dog's coat. The dog thought he was getting a treat and looked thoroughly disappointed when she pulled her hand away and left no goodie behind.

"Yes, I've heard about Ellen's shampoo," I said. "Thank you for the tissue."

Lola looked at me with scrunched brows. "Why are you familiar with dog shampoo? Or is that crow getting his own special salon time now?"

"No, although Kingston would probably love to be primped and pampered. Of course, he's not a big fan of baths. James and I were on the beach last night—" I was about to explain my knowledge of dog shampoo but Lola was instantly riveted to our beach picnic.

"Oh, that's right. How was it? Romantic?" she asked with a flutter of her lashes and a simpering smile.

"Stop that. James and I enjoy our trips to the beach. And yes, as a matter of fact, it was rather romantic. Except when Bear sprayed us with sand and salt water. But it was nice. I was about to tell you about the dog shampoo but forget it. Let's just look for Terry."

"Yes?" a voice came out from behind one of the tiny portable trailers. A head of white hair followed. "Did someone call me?" Terry had switched her bright blue glasses for black sunglasses. "Lacey, you're here." She came out from behind the trailer wiping her hands on a work apron. "I was just tossing some trash." Her shoulders deflated some as she looked at my hands clutching nothing but a tissue. "I was expecting you to have the arrangements finished. I need to set up the stage—"

"Yes, I brought them. In fact, I placed them on the stage before walking through the event to find you. They are very tall. I think you'll be pleased. The paw print ribbon was a great idea, adds a touch of whimsy."

"Wonderful, I can't wait to see them." She led us back down the pathway. A blue vintage teardrop camper was being towed up to the vacant spot closest to the stage. The side of the trailer was painted with a picture of a cocker spaniel. The name Belvedere was painted in purple beneath it.

"Oh, there's Avery Hinkle." Terry turned back to me. "Just a moment. I need to tell her where to hook up her electricity." Lola and I waited while Terry went up to the window of the truck pulling the camper. It was hard to see clearly through the tinted windshield, but it was easy to spot the silhouette of a dog sitting regally in the passenger seat. The backseat was filled with items that were probably for the show. A tall man was scrunched in beside the pile of things.

"Boy, it seems this dog show stuff goes to their heads a bit. That dog is sitting as if he's used to being chauffeured around like a prince, while the humans sit in the back surrounded by his doggie fineries and toiletries," Lola said quietly, considering we were surrounded by pampered pups and their owners.

I leaned closer to her. "Well, with a name like Belvedere."

Terry returned quickly. "All right then, we can continue. I couldn't very well let Avery Hinkle search around for the electrical hookups," she said as if we should know this famous Avery Hinkle.

Lola was never one to just let things pass. "Is she some sort of big shot in the dog world?"

I elbowed Lola lightly but knew my admonishment was only going to egg her on.

Terry looked slightly taken aback and utterly shocked that we had no idea who Avery Hinkle was. "Avery is, for lack of a better phrase," she said with a grin, "top dog around here. Her cocker spaniel, Belvedere, wins every show."

"Sort of takes away from the fun, doesn't it? I mean why does anybody show up if they're just going to hand the ribbon to Belvedere?" Lola was feeling ornery. She was apparently practicing for her mother's arrival.

Terry sputtered over her answer and looked both annoyed and yet slightly intrigued about Lola's questions. "Well, I suppose there is always a chance that a finer dog is entered and steals the show . . . so to speak. My, my, I'm certainly talking in puns today."

We reached the stage and the sunflower arrangements. I was just as happy not to continue our silly conversation.

"I love them," Terry cheered. "You're right, the ribbon is perfect. I know just where to place them."

"Wonderful. I'm glad you're happy with them." I pulled her receipt out of my pocket. "You paid in advance so there's nothing left to do except say 'have a terrific and successful show'."

"Thank you so much, and I'll be sure to pass on the good word about Pink's Flowers," she added.

"That would be greatly appreciated."

Lola and I headed across the field. "Good thing she had already paid in advance with your snide remarks about the dog show," I said as we headed toward the walking path.

"It wasn't snide," she countered. "It seemed like a logical question." We passed the famous duo of Avery and Belvedere as she said it. Avery, a curvy woman in slightly undersized clothes, was pulling a royal blue banner out of a thick plastic bag that was dotted with paw prints, just like the ribbons on the sunflower arrangements. A tall, broad shouldered man, the backseat occupant, left his task of setting up a dog pen to help Avery unfurl her banner. It read Belvedere, 2018 Chesterton Grand Show Champion. Many of the other competitors were watching the whole scene, some with awe and some with envy, it seemed.

Lola and I headed along the pathway.

"I wonder if she just changes the year each time or if she buys a whole new banner," Lola said. "I still say it must be a pretty dull contest if everyone already knows the winner."

"I see your point. But then, like Terry said, you never know when a new champion is just waiting to upset the status quo."

CHAPTER 4

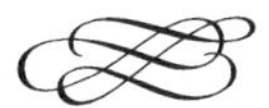

Lola and I had planned to leave the park and stop for a bite to eat somewhere on the way back to our shops, but one of the food vendors was selling yummy looking taco salads so we ordered two, with the works, including a nice dollop of guacamole, and hung out for awhile.

I had to use my self-learned skills of blocking out the extraneous fragrances so I could enjoy the marvelous salad. I had such a terrible time ignoring outside smells when I was a kid that I could hardly ever finish a meal. I was so thin my classmates called me a stick figure. Slowly, and with considerable concentration and effort, I learned how to turn off my hyper sense of smell so I could enjoy food.

Most of the picnic benches were filled with people working to set up the show, and visitors already swarming the park to get a look at the competitors. Lola and I found a spot under a tree near the mobile dog salon trailer. Coincidentally enough, Ellen Joyner, the woman Briggs and I had met at the beach the night before, was walking her very stylish poodle up the steps of the trailer.

"Ellen, I'm over here," a woman called across the way. The

woman in her mid to late twenties with thin hair that was clipped back from her cute, round face was being hurried along by two French bulldogs.

"Melody, what are you doing? I thought you'd be busy grooming," Ellen called to her.

Melody was slightly winded when she reached the steps. "I decided to offer my services as dog walker for the show," she explained to Ellen.

Ellen glowered down at the dogs. "Are those the Crampton's dogs?" She glanced around the park. "I haven't been unlucky enough to run into Horace and Belinda yet."

"They only just arrived. They asked me to watch Hamilton and Caprese while they set up."

"Did she just say that bulldog's name was Caprese?" Lola whispered. "Isn't that a salad with mozzarella and tomato? What a strange name for a dog."

I glanced at her. "Said the woman who named her dog Late Bloomer."

"Yes but there's a whole history behind the name. Bloomer took a long time to, you know, bloom. Naming a dog after a salad is just silly." She lifted her bowl. "But there's nothing silly about these salads. Best I've had in a long time." She plucked out a chip and dipped it directly into the guacamole.

I copied her maneuver. "I agree. These are delicious."

Lola and I continued to nibble silently on our salads, enjoying each bite while we watched the activity at the dog show. Melody placed the two bulldogs in a dog pen and hung their leashes on a hook outside the door of the trailer. The two women and the poodle went inside.

Just minutes later, an older couple, presumably the Cramptons because they headed straight to the pen to retrieve their bulldogs, arrived at the trailer. The man had a black beard with sprigs of gray and a belly that hung proudly over his belt buckle. The woman was far more fit and moved energetically and efficiently, reminding me a touch of Elsie. Only Mrs. Crampton had ginger hair tucked under a bright blue cap.

They didn't seem pleased about finding their dogs sitting unattended in a pen. Mrs. Crampton stuck her hands on her hips (again reminding me of Elsie). She turned sharply to Mr. Crampton. "I certainly didn't pay her twenty dollars to leave my babies sitting alone out here," she said with enough force that it carried across to where Lola and I were standing. "I'm going to have to have a word with Melody."

"Now, Belinda," Mr. Crampton said in a much gentler tone but his baritone voice still carried. "She probably had to go inside and help a customer."

"Aren't we customers? We paid her money to walk the dogs, but I don't see my dogs walking," Belinda snapped.

"Who knew we'd have a soap opera to watch while we ate our salads." Lola plowed her fork into the bowl for another bite but kept her gaze riveted on the unfolding drama.

The Cramptons left their pooches in the pen while they marched up the portable steps to the trailer door. Belinda knocked sharply but then didn't wait to be invited in before swinging open the door.

Unfortunately, their voices and the discussion were muffled within the walls of the trailer.

"Darn, now we're not going to know how the story ends," Lola said.

"Probably wouldn't be all that gratifying of an ending anyhow. Are you ready to head back to Port Danby?" I asked.

"I suppose so."

I walked a few feet to a trash can and tossed my mostly empty bowl. Lola did the same. Right then, the light door on the trailer swung open hard enough to smack the outside wall. The Cramptons marched down the steps looking none too pleased with their visit. Lola and I walked toward the path which took us closer to the couple, close enough to hear Belinda complaining. Only she was no longer griping about Melody and the lack of exercise for her dogs. She had some rather choice words for Ellen Joyner, the woman with the poodle.

"Ellen Joyner is a conniving witch. She has some nerve. Wasn't she just acting the innocent. I'm sure she saw Melody walking Hamilton and Caprese, and she rushed right over with that smug, over-styled poodle to get in the way of the walk."

That was the last we heard as we headed along the pathway to the parking lot.

Lola glanced back at the angry couple. "Who knew dog shows were a hot bed of drama."

CHAPTER 5

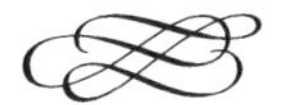

"Your shop door is propped open." I startled Lola out of her short cat nap.

She sat up and peered through the front windshield. It took her a second to shake off the grogginess. "What the heck?" She slumped back down. "Ugh, the black cloud has landed and cast its dreary shadow on Port Danby. Cynthia and John have arrived."

I swept into the only parking spot on the street, just a block from our shops. "Guess we took too long for lunch."

"I'm blaming it on the Cramptons. That's either the best or the worst surname in the world. At least now Mom will be too busy questioning me about closing the shop midday to comment on my attire."

I glanced over at her faded t-shirt. Lola had the finest collection of vintage rock t-shirts but the Stone Temple Pilots one was particularly shabby. If I didn't know any better, I'd guess that she chose that t-shirt just to annoy her mom.

"Well, good luck," I said as I turned off the engine.

She sat up straighter. "Wait, I've got a great idea. Come into the shop with me. Mom always puts on her best face for visitors. She might even tone down her first few gripes about my appearance if you're standing next to me." She peered quickly my direction. "Or maybe that's a mistake. You look far more fresh and pretty and girlie. The comparison is too drastic."

I turned in my seat. "Normally, I would thank someone for calling me fresh and pretty and girlie, only I sensed just the tiniest bit of derision as you said it so I won't be thanking you. It seems to me that if you knew your mom was going to complain about the way you're dressed, you could have at least pulled out one of your nicer t-shirts."

Lola stared down at the shirt. "Nothing wrong with my t-shirt." She looked up at me. "So are you going to be a good friend and escort me into my shop or not?"

I grabbed my purse from the backseat. "Fine. I'll walk you in —coward."

We walked across to Lola's Antiques. Her parents' voices floated out to us before we stepped inside. Lola stopped and took a deep breath. "Here we go." She strode in. "Hey, guys, you got in early," she said cheerily.

Lola's parents didn't look like your average, everyday mom and pop. They looked altogether more worldly than Stanley and Peggy Pinkerton. My parents looked as if they'd lived an easy, ordinary life in the suburbs, both a little paunchy with clothing that was neither contemporary nor outdated. Lola's dad, John Button, had graying temples. With his crisply tailored white shirt with rolled sleeves and khaki shorts, it looked as if he was about to go out on a safari. He was a thick haired ginger like his daughter, but his skin had a dark coppery tone as if he'd spent the last month on the French Riviera, which he quite possibly had. Cynthia Button, Lola's mom, had dyed her hair a deep henna color. This afternoon she was wearing an exotic dress made of gauzy batik fabric.

Both parents rushed right over for hugs and kisses hello. For a brief second, it seemed Lola was happy to see them. (Not that she would ever admit it.)

Cynthia pulled away first and flashed a gracious grin my direction. "Lacey, right?"

I walked forward. "Yes, we met briefly on your last visit." I put out my hand but she pulled me into a hug.

"I'm so glad Lola has you for a friend. She talks so much about you."

"We have become very close, and I'm glad to have her too."

Cynthia stepped back. She turned an admiring gaze toward Lola. "Your hair looks so pretty with all those curls, sweetie."

Lola's mouth dropped. It seemed she was unprepared for a compliment. "Thanks," she said hesitantly. Then she squinted suspiciously at her mom, waiting, apparently, for the other shoe to drop. Which it did.

"I suppose it just looks better because you don't have one of those silly old man hats pulled down over it."

"Ah, there it is." Lola looked at her dad. "Almost thought you grabbed the wrong woman at the airport."

"Oh, don't be silly, Lola," Cynthia piped up before John could respond. Not that he seemed to know how to respond.

"Your mom and I had a long trip." John finally spoke up. "We're going to head home to shower and take a nap. We just wanted to stop by the shop first and say hello." Late Bloomer sat at his feet and stared up at him. He patted the dog's head. "We can take Bloomer with us."

"Yes, sweetie, we were a little surprised to find the shop closed. You might have missed some customers." Cynthia stepped over to a walnut buffet and straightened a few of the china cups Lola had displayed on its shelves. "It's not good business."

Lola wasn't exaggerating. I was beginning to think even my mom couldn't go toe to toe with Cynthia.

"I have to eat lunch, don't I? I think it would be even worse business to leave the shop open with no one minding the store." Lola grinned at her.

"Oh, Lola, you are being extra silly this afternoon. Maybe you should be the one to go home and take a nap," Cynthia mused.

"Sounds good to me," she said. "Does that mean you two will be in charge? After all, I don't really get days off for things like naps." I was about to mention her nap on the way home from Chesterton but thought better of it.

"We told you to hire an assistant," John said.

"I tried a few but there aren't many good ones." Lola stepped over to the buffet and moved the china cups back to where she'd originally placed them. Cynthia decided to ignore it.

"Speaking of assistants—" Cynthia turned to me. Her skin was virtually flawless. I wondered how many European spas she frequented during their travels. "How is your floral assistant?" She said it with just enough distaste that I instantly felt sorry for Ryder. It seemed he wasn't going to have as easy a time of it as I'd predicted.

Fortunately, it took no effort to sing his praises. "Ryder is the best assistant anyone could ask for. He's talented and knowledgeable. Customers adore him. Everyone adores him, in fact. He's going to go far in life."

"Well, we can't wait to meet him," Cynthia said, but I questioned the sincerity in her tone.

"Yes, all in good time." Lola started walking them to the door. "Like you said, time for naps. I'm afraid the refrigerator is sort of empty. I haven't been to the store, but I'll pick up some pizza on the way home."

Cynthia stopped to admire a Victorian chair. "Sweetie, this chair needs dusting. I know we like to see patina on these old pieces but dust doesn't really say old. It says dirty."

That was my cue to leave. I swept past Lola, who seemed to be deciding whether this battle was worth fighting or whether she should save energy for future fights.

"It was nice seeing you both again," I said cheerily as I walked past.

"Yes, you too," Cynthia called as I reached the door. I walked outside and hurried across the street.

Ryder was finishing potting some marigolds when I walked inside.

"Run," I said, "Run and don't look back."

Ryder's face blanched, and I felt guilty for teasing him. "I'm kidding. The parents have arrived and let's just say, Lola wasn't exaggerating."

He dried off his hands. "Poor Lo-lo. *Poor me*," he said more emphatically. "I think I'll go grab some lunch. I can't meet them on an empty stomach."

"Good point. You'll need all your strength. Hurry though. Lola was trying to get them out the door, only Cynthia seemed intent on inspecting for dust."

"Oh man, that's going to leave Lola in knot. I'm heading out now, and I think I'll follow your earlier warning. I'm going to run down to the diner and not look back."

Ryder dashed out the door and headed toward the diner. I was feeling oddly homesick for my own mom. The shop was empty so I pulled out my phone.

"Lacey?" she always answered with a questioning tone as if she thought possibly someone else had decided to use my phone to call her.

"Who else?" I said back. "What's up, Mom? How are you guys doing?"

"Why do you sound so nasal? Do you have a cold?"

"I sound nasal? Well, that's a pretty way to sound. I don't have a cold," I said.

"What's new?" she asked, without answering my questions. "Is there anything wrong? Are you still dating James? Is the flower shop doing all right? You could always go back into the perfume industry if the flower thing didn't work out."

I smiled into the phone and briefly wondered if Cynthia Button and Peggy Pinkerton would get along. "Let's see. Nothing is new, except I did buy a new pair of sandals. Nothing is wrong. Yes, I'm dating James. Yes, the flower shop is fine. And I don't want to go back to the perfume industry, so hopefully, the flower *thing* will keep working."

"Well, that's nice, dear. I didn't expect to hear from you today."

"I know, Mom. I just missed you and thought I'd ring you up."

CHAPTER 6

I pulled the dish of lasagna out of the oven and placed it on the trivet. "*Now,* this is my first attempt at lasagna. It's my mom's recipe and it's delicious. Or at least it is when she makes it."

Briggs turned away from Kingston. The two had been having a short *conversation,* although it was fairly one-sided. "I'm sure yours will be delicious too," he said. "Besides, I'm so hungry, I'm even looking forward to those vegan cookies Elsie sent over." He stared down at the plate of trail mix cookies. "Are you sure they're really vegan or did she sneak some butter and eggs in? Because I have to say, they smell great."

"Yes, they are vegan and you'll love them. I told you the woman never did *kicks.* She's planning on creating an entire line of vegan treats for the bakery."

"Jeez, Les," Briggs lamented, "what have you and your high cholesterol done to the rest of us?"

"You have been spoiled with dairy and meat, sir. Now sit down and eat this meaty and cheesy lasagna."

Briggs pulled out a chair and sat. He looked weary from a long day at work. I sensed that something had him a little distracted.

I sat across from him and served us each a portion of lasagna. "Long strings of cheese," I said. "That's a good sign."

"What sign? That I'll soon be joining Les in the high rolling cholesterol club?" He dropped a napkin on his lap.

"Now I'm feeling guilty for feeding you this heart disease meal. But I worked for hours." I pushed the plate his direction. "So eat every last bite."

Briggs sat forward and picked up his fork. The crease over his brow was more pronounced than usual.

"Are you on a tough case?" I asked. "You look like you're worried about something." I sat forward excitedly. "Did someone get murdered? Do you need my sniffer?"

A half smile formed on his face. "Most people don't ask about a murder with so much enthusiasm, but no, no one died. I don't need your cute little sniffer on this case. We're just waiting for a large shipment of drugs to be delivered to a group we've had under surveillance for months. Activity seems to be ratcheting up, so I think we'll see some action this week. Then we can make arrests."

"That sounds dangerous," I said it lightly. I knew he didn't want me worrying about him, but it was impossible to ignore that Briggs had a dangerous job. I couldn't let myself think about it too much or I'd wind myself into a twist. "You should take over for Ryder when he leaves on his world adventure. Flower arranging is much safer."

He finished a bite and nodded approvingly at the food. "Good lasagna. You might be a flower arranger, but you manage to get into plenty of sticky situations."

"Only when I'm on a case with you. When I'm in my flowery world, it's all petals and perfumes. Speaking of perfumes, Lola and I delivered the sunflower arrangements to the dog show in Chesterton. The fragrances floating around those masterfully groomed dogs put ole' Samantha into overdrive." I tapped my nose. "Almost couldn't taste the taco salads we ordered for lunch. I saw our friend with the poodle too."

His brows bunched together as he tried to figure out what poodle friend I was referring to.

"The lady from last night. At the beach. Remember? Bear made a new friend."

"Oh yeah, the lady who makes dog shampoo." He went back to his meal. The lines reappeared on his face.

I put down my fork. "James," I said quietly. "Should I be worried?"

"No, not at all. I'm sure it's just as delicious as your mom's," he teased.

I reached my foot across to tap his toe. "Stop. You know what I mean. What team are you working with? It's not Officer Chinmoor, is it? He's a nice guy and all, but I hardly see him in a big drug sting operation."

Briggs shook his head. "No, I've got a team from Mayfield working the case with me. Chinmoor is holding down the fort around here. And he's getting better at, you know, policing."

"I'm sure he is but I feel better knowing you've got a Mayfield team working with you." Suddenly, the cheesy lasagna didn't look as tempting.

Briggs peeked up and noticed I was just picking at my plate. "Lacey, you don't need to be worried. This is not my first big drug bust, and I doubt it will be the last." He reached across and took hold of my hand. "You aren't going to get rid of me that easy."

I only half laughed. He saw that his comment wasn't helpful. "I'm sorry, baby. I won't tease you anymore," he said in that deep, mellow tone that always sent a wave of warmth through me, especially when he threw in the word *baby*.

He sat back in his chair and picked up his fork. "This really is delicious. Might even have a second helping. I'll probably be too full to try the vegan cookies so when Elsie asks—"

"No way, buddy. You're going to try a trail mix cookie, and I think you are going to be pleasantly surprised."

His lashes lifted and he peered across the table at me. "Oh? Does that mean you already ate one?"

I bit my lip coyly. "A cookie might have landed in my hand while I was preparing the lasagna. It was hard work and I needed nourishment. They are crunchy and delicious. So prepare to be amazed."

"All right, if you say so. I'll try and keep an open mind. I just hope Les knows the sacrifices the rest of us are making on his behalf."

CHAPTER 7

For a second time in less than twenty-four hours, I was heading to the Chesterton Dog Show. Elsie's niece, Britney, had planned to sell Elsie's popular dog treats at the show, but she had come home so late from a date with Dash the night before, she woke with a headache. Britney said she couldn't stand in the sun all day, so the task fell to Elsie. It was going to be another reason for Elsie to complain about Britney's relationship with Dash, a rather tenuous and one-sided pairing that caused Britney enough anxiety that Elsie had begun to dislike Dash. I worked hard not to get involved in the matter at all. I was too close to members of both parties, so to speak. However, deep down, I hoped the whole thing would just end amiably. I was sure those were high hopes because Britney, who was in every way a superior, independent and talented young woman, had a terrible weak spot when it came to my handsome, charismatic friend and neighbor, Dashwood Vanhouten.

Elsie drove like she lived, fast and efficiently. She turned sharply around a corner and, unfortunately, started on the topic of Britney and Dash. "Well, she's going to regret staying out so late. I had three orders for party cupcakes to fill today, so Brit is going to be busy baking and decorating. Selling dog treats at the park will be much easier. In fact, I look forward to the break," she said, but I wasn't totally convinced she meant it. Even though Britney was a highly skilled pastry chef, Elsie still liked to inspect and approve everything that left her shop. "All I know is that Dash has made a mess of things. (It wasn't the first time I'd heard her say it.) I'd finally found a great assistant. Britney was going to be such an asset to the business, all while learning the skills and ins and outs of running a bakery, then Dash had to step into the bakery with his thick blond hair and green eyes. He's not even all that handsome," she added.

I raised a brow her direction.

"All right," she said. "He's very handsome, if you like that sort of Hollywood leading man kind of thing."

I suppressed a laugh and searched quickly for a different topic. "Oh wow, I forgot to tell you, James ate three of those vegan cookies last night. He kept saying, I'll bet Elsie snuck in some butter and eggs. How else could they taste so good?"

Elsie adjusted her sunglasses. The sky was clear. It was going to be a bright, hot day at the park. "James is just like Les. My brother refuses to believe that foods without butter, cheese and meat are real food." She chuckled. "Yesterday, Les tried to negotiate a new deal for the diet I've put him on. He told me he'd eat healthy all week, then go hog wild on the weekends with nachos and beer."

I scooted down in the seat a bit. Elsie sensed my *shrinkage*. She glanced over at me. "Well, well, I guess I can see where this new idea came from," she said.

I shot back up since the cat was out of the bag on Les's inspirational source. "In my defense, I didn't tell him to go hog wild. He looked so miserable yesterday as he picked through that bowl of vegetables."

"Was Les walking around town with that veggie bowl?" Elsie

pulled into the parking lot of the Chesterton Dog Show. There were very few vacant parking spots left. The park itself was overflowing with people and dogs.

"Not around town. He came into the flower shop because he thought the healthy lunch might go down a little easier with friends. I'm afraid we weren't much help. Then Lola came in to lament her parents' imminent arrival. I exchanged a few words with Mom and Dad Button, by the way, and I think Lola is going to have a tough week."

"Cynthia is a little sharp around the edges," Elsie said, "but I've always liked John. I still remember when they opened that antique store across the street. Lola was still in diapers, with hair as red as fire and a spirit to match."

I laughed. "I'll bet she was a handful."

Elsie parked a good distance away from the area where the dogs and stage were set up. A line of vendor tables had been organized along the walking path. Elsie handed me a box that was filled to the brim with cellophane wrapped dog treats. She pulled out another box with a tablecloth that was printed with puppies and three silver trays for displaying the goodies.

It seemed Elsie was the last vendor to arrive. She had reserved a table. The show organizer, Terry, I presumed, had placed a folded placard that read Elsie's Sugar and Spice Bakery on the table. We were right next to Viv's Pet Boutique, where a thirty something woman with a rhinestone studded t-shirt was hanging sparkly dog collars on a rack.

"Morning," the woman chirruped. "I'm Vivian and of course you are Elsie. I've been to your bakery many times, as you can probably tell." She patted her slight paunch, then pulled a few business cards out of a display. "Here's my card. Call me sometime. I would love to sell some of your custom dog treats in my boutique. I'm right here in Chesterton."

Elsie and I each took a card. I now had two business cards for dog supplies, even though I had no dog. Elsie forced a grin. "Not sure if I'd have enough time to make extra treats but sure, we can talk sometime." She stuck the business card in her pocket. I knew Elsie well enough to know that she would never consider the notion. She liked too much to be in control. I personally thought the idea had merit.

I lifted the card. "Thank you, my boyfriend has a dog and—" I motioned to a black collar with punk rocker silver studs. "I might have to buy him that very rock and rollish collar. I think Bear would like it."

"How fun," Vivian said. She seemed to be one of those cheery types, which I didn't mind, but she would probably get on Elsie's nerves quickly. "Your boyfriend's name is Bear?" she asked.

Elsie snickered as she busied herself setting up the table.

"Actually, the dog's name is Bear. He'd look great in the collar, but I'll have to think about it. Nice meeting you."

Vivian's attention was diverted away from our conversation as a small group of people wandered along the vendor tables, stopping to check out products and all looking toward one person for her opinion and approval. It seemed Avery, the woman with the champion cocker spaniel, had quite a fan club. The other women shuffled along next to her, all vying for her attention. It reminded me of the popular girls in high school who were always being followed by a set of groupies, all waiting for a sliver of attention.

Vivian waved to Avery before she even reached her table. The tall man who had been scrunched in the backseat with her dog show equipment tagged along with the group but seemed more interested in his breakfast burrito than in the wares being sold along the path. He was wearing an orange shirt advertising Hart's Feed and Grain. He looked like the kind of guy who spent the day tossing heavy bales of hay around a barn.

"I guess she's sort of the queen around here," I muttered Vivian's direction.

"Who Avery? Yes, absolutely. She has a lot of clout. One mention on her blog and your products can go through the roof." She pointed out a pair of paw socks, cute and dainty with little stars. "Avery once mentioned that she had bought Belvedere a pair of my special paw socks to keep his feet warm in winter. I sold out of every pair and had a waiting list a mile long."

"Wow, that definitely is clout. That tall man walking next to her, is that her husband?"

Vivian glanced my way. "That's Barrett Hart. His family owns Hart's Feed and Grain. They have the best selection of dog food in the county. They aren't married. Just dating."

"Yes, I've heard of Hart's Feed and Grain. Well, I came to help, so I suppose I should get to it. Nice talking to you." I returned my attention to our table.

Elsie handed me a box of cat shaped dog cookies. "Put these on that tray," she instructed.

"Yes, m'am," I answered back. "Although, as a cat lover, I'm not sure how I feel about these cat shaped treats. They seem to be crossing the line of political correctness," I teased.

Elsie laughed. "Just make sure all the pointy ears are going in the same direction. They look better that way."

In the distance, a voice came through a loudspeaker announcing the winner of the toy breed class. Applause followed and a few of the surrounding vendors, including Vivian, clapped and cheered, even though we were far from the action on stage.

Vivian smiled my direction. "Juju Bean is one of my clients. The cutest little silky terrier ever." She pointed out her extra bling-worthy dog collars. "She's wearing one of my rhinestone creations for the show. They don't usually like extravagant collars in the show, but they make an exception for the toy breeds. They're so cute when they're all dressed up."

"I'm sure Juju Bean wore your collar with pride," I said and then turned back to a slight scowl from Elsie. She motioned to my half filled tray, letting me know I needed to stop socializing and start working. Sometimes I wondered if the relationship with Dash was truly the thing that was giving Britney anxiety.

Avery stopped at Vivian's table. She and her followers spent a good deal of time checking out the collars and socks and other baubles displayed on the table. In the meantime, we were gathering our own crowd of customers, both two legged and four legged. It seemed the two legged were somewhat disappointed to arrive at the Sugar and Spice Bakery table and find only dog treats. It dawned on Elsie that she'd made a mistake by not bringing along some of her people cookies too.

"Pink, I hate to ask this of you, but do you mind if I race back to the bakery for some real cookies?"

"Probably a good idea because I get the feeling some of our customers are willing to nibble on the peanut butter dog treats just to get a bite of one of Elsie's cookies."

She pulled her purse out from under the table and put it on her shoulder. "I'll be right back with chocolate chip and lemon cookies."

"Oh, and bring some of those caramel ones, the ones that require a great deal of finger licking," I said.

"It might be too hot out here for those. They'll melt into a gooey mess."

"Your point?" I said with an impish grin. "Besides, I was requesting those just for me. Stop in at the flower shop to make sure Ryder isn't being overwhelmed with orders. I wasn't expecting any wedding clients today, but you never know when one will walk through the door."

"Right, check on Ryder and some chocolate chip, lemon and a few caramel for my hardworking assistant. I'll be back in half an hour."

CHAPTER 8

Elsie returned with the cookies, and after finger licking my way through a caramel one, I wandered over to the show stage. The various category champions had been chosen, and it was time for the grand champion to be named. The blue ribbon winners from each category had to strut around the stage and stand at attention on a table to be examined for breed perfection. As I reached the stage, the adorable silky terrier was just leaving, and the highly anticipated Belvedere was about to make his entrance.

Avery walked onto stage but looked a tad less confident than I'd seen her when she strolled the park with her entourage. As much as she tried to keep the straight posture and easy walk of a dog handler, she seemed to be struggling to get Belvedere to cooperate. Belvedere was a stunning blue roan cocker spaniel with wavy ears and a lush coat. Unfortunately, a mouthful of something had his snout and jaw moving up and down and in every direction.

The crowd held a collective gasp. The woman next to me leaned closer. "If I didn't know any better, I'd say that dog has his snout filled with peanut butter," she muttered.

I nodded. "You're right. Seems kind of strange she would feed him that just before he went on stage."

"There's no way Avery gave him that peanut butter," she said, still in a low voice. The entire crowd had fallen silent. It seemed breaths were being held as Avery struggled to lead her preoccupied dog around the stage. The dog was still working on the peanut butter as Avery lifted him onto the table for the judge's inspection. Avery looked beyond despondent and, at the same time, a little hot under the collar. A sheen of red anger seemed to be rising along her neck and over her round cheeks.

The judge, an older woman with short gray hair and a pink blouse, seemed both amused and confused. Belvedere just couldn't relax his jaw enough to stand still for the judging. They were dismissed fairly quickly, a gesture that sent a low moan of shock through the onlookers. I wasn't a dog show expert, but it seemed the grand champion was about to give up his title.

Avery marched off the steps and headed back to her trailer. Her boyfriend, hands in pockets, shuffled reluctantly behind, keeping a bit of distance between him and the angry dog handler.

Ellen Joyner and her poodle were called onto the stage next. Pebbles, the standard poodle, trotted proudly around the stage, her gray pompoms bouncing spritely with each step. She stood as still as a statue for the judge. The woman took her judging duties very seriously as she checked Pebbles' teeth and back and tail. The crowd seemed impressed.

I glanced at the woman who I'd chatted briefly with. She was wearing a green cap and a pair of dog paw print earrings. "I suppose Belvedere's misfortune is going to be Pebbles' good luck. She is a very striking dog," I said.

The woman nodded. "Yes, Ellen and Avery have been rivals for a long time. Ellen has wanted this win badly, but Belvedere is a hard dog to beat. Not today, however. I think you're right. Looks like the judge is going to pick Pebbles."

A few of the final contestants strutted around stage. To me, they were all wonderful dogs but then I loved animals in every shape, color and size. Apparently, showing that she was a good sport, Avery and her boyfriend, Barrett, returned to hear the judge announce the winner.

The cute little judge in her pink blouse, looking as if she was about to announce the winner of the presidency, walked up to the microphone. A few minutes passed as Terry rushed on stage to lower the mic so that the judge could reach it.

"The runner up for the 2019 Chesterton Dog Show is Bailey, the basset hound." A long eared, droopy cheeked basset hound climbed up the steps on his stumpy legs with his owner. He was adorable and wrinkly and seemed to understand that he had just won a ribbon. His owner, a man with a long ponytail and sandals, leaned down to pet the dog and give him a treat. He stood off to the side as the judge stretched up to the microphone again. Terry carried over a large blue ribbon and silver trophy complete with handles and fancy engraving.

"And the grand champion of the Chesterton Dog Show is Pebbles, the standard poodle."

Aside from Ellen's squeals of delight, the first sound from the audience was more of a gasp than a cheer. Slowly though, the applause began, and people started cheering for the poodle and her beaming owner.

Pebbles sat still as a statue as the ribbon was attached to her collar. Ellen walked up to the microphone. Her voice wavered from the excitement. "As most of you know, I've been working toward this win for many years. I knew Pebbles was going to bring home that blue ribbon one day."

"You cheated!" Avery screamed from the audience. The crowd fell silent.

Barrett put his hand on Avery's shoulder as she moved toward the stage, but she shrugged it off. Avery pointed up at Ellen. "You sabotaged Belvedere's performance by giving him peanut butter. Don't deny it. I know it was you."

Ellen looked around the crowd for support, but Avery was the big fish in the group and it seemed people were ready to come to her defense. "Cheater," someone yelled. "Saboteur," another person said.

Ellen rolled her lips in an attempt not to cry. "No," she said weakly into the microphone. "No, I didn't. I never went near Belvedere. It wasn't me," she insisted. I didn't know the woman well, but she seemed to be sincere in her denial. Still, she was the person to benefit the most from Belvedere's peanut butter fiasco.

To add to Ellen's misery, the Cramptons, who were obviously not fans, walked up to comfort Avery. Belinda pointed angrily up at the stage. "Pebbles does not deserve that ribbon because you cheated."

Ellen clutched her trophy and Pebbles' leash and ran off the stage sobbing. It was a sad, unsettling ending to the event, but Terry forged ahead. She walked up on stage and forced a smile as she leaned down to the microphone. "We're going to play some music through the loudspeakers if anyone is interested in dancing. We'll be serving root beer floats too, so stick around and have some doggone fun." Her enthusiasm was as forced as the grin on her face. It seemed the final award had drawn a cloud over the entire event.

I walked back to Elsie's table to help her sell off the rest of her goodies so we could head back to Port Danby.

CHAPTER 9

It had been a long morning and afternoon. Elsie had sold off the last dog treat and after a contentious finale, the competitors and vendors were packing up to head home. There was little to pack up at our table, trays were stacked and decorative doilies brushed off for reuse. Elsie still had a stack of business cards so she wandered off to hand them out to some of the visitors.

Vivian, who had been a congenial neighbor throughout the day, even watching our table when Elsie and I stepped away for a bite to eat, needed some help packing up. I lent her a hand.

"This is so nice of you." She handed me a box. "If you could just stack the dog socks in here, I'll start packing up the collars. I feel like I didn't sell as many as I expected. I think the shocking end to the show put a dreary mood on the shoppers."

"It was an unusual ending, that's for sure," I noted.

"Vivian," a somewhat distraught voice said.

Vivian and I both looked up from our task. Melody was looking downright baffled. She was holding Pebbles, the champion poodle, on a leash.

"Why do you have Pebbles?" Vivian asked. "Where's Ellen?"

"That's what I was about to ask you." Pebbles licked Melody's hand. It was the first time I'd seen the dog do anything except stand or sit at attention. Melody pulled her hand away from the dog's snout. "Ellen brought Pebbles to me right after the show. She was upset." Melody shrugged slightly. "Understandably so. She asked if I could give Pebbles a walk and comb out while she rested. She said the whole thing on stage had given her a headache. She didn't want to leave Pebbles in her pen because she was worried Avery might do something to her. I haven't seen Ellen since. I knocked on her trailer and no answer. I've been wandering around looking for her. I was hoping you had seen her."

Vivian shook her head. "I haven't seen her since this morning."

"I have to say, I haven't seen her since she left the stage with her trophy and ribbon," I said. "Maybe she fell asleep," I suggested.

"I thought that might be the case, so I knocked very hard and called her name. No answer. Well, thanks anyway. I guess I'll just keep walking Pebbles around until I find her. She'll have to show up at some point. She would never just leave without her precious dog." Melody walked away with the champion poodle in tow.

"That's strange," Vivian noted. "I wonder where Ellen could be. I felt really sorry for her after what happened. I wasn't at the stage, but some of the other dog owners came by to tell me all about the peanut butter sabotage and the scene Avery made when Ellen and Pebbles won. Ellen has been taking the backseat to Avery's and Belvedere's rock star fame for several years. It's always Belvedere first and Pebbles as the runner up. I guess she finally just cracked and decided she had to have that first place ribbon. Just doesn't seem like something she would do."

"Then maybe it wasn't Ellen," I suggested. "Maybe somewhere along the way, Avery has stepped on someone else's toes or, in this case, paws."

"I suppose. Avery has mostly fans, but I'm sure there are more than a few people envious of her success." Vivian closed up the box of dog socks. "Guess we'll never know for sure, which is too bad because that means Pebbles' win will always be tainted. Some people will not even see it as a legitimate win. Poor Ellen," she lamented as she rolled up some stylish dog leashes.

I was more than ready to head back to Port Danby, but Elsie was busy talking with a group of people. I knew she didn't get many free days away from the bakery, so I decided not to hurry her away from her conversation. I pulled my purse out from under our table to glance at my phone. There were several texts from Lola.

"It would have been much less aggravating to just be abducted by those darn aliens," said the first text.

The second one was more detailed. "The mad woman is actually rearranging the entire store. She thinks I'm showcasing the wrong items. I've been running the place without her for two years but she's the one who knows which items should be showcased. Talk about a self-confidence shredder."

Her third text was directed at me, no doubt because I hadn't commented on the first two. "I'm replacing you as my best friend because I'm in meltdown mode and you are ignoring me. So there. I might go across the street and sit with Kingston. He loves me no matter what."

I wrote back. "I've been helping Elsie sell her dog treats. We were swamped with customers, and my phone was in my purse. Sorry I missed the meltdown, but I'll try to be around for the next melt. And Kingston would love a visit from his favorite person."

A text came back quickly. "Yes, Kingston listened to my rant for about three minutes before getting sidetracked by a pair of sparrows in the tree outside the shop window. Surprisingly, I felt better after our little chat. Then I went back across to the antique shop and all the tension returned."

"Sorry about that, bestie," I texted back. "If that's what we still are . . . hopefully."

"I suppose I can forgive you this time. Especially because your crow was a decent stand in. Got to go. Apparently we are going to spend a joyous hour in the storeroom looking for 'ignored treasures'."

"Good luck with that," I texted back. Elsie returned just as we finished the text conversation.

"Everything all right back on Harbor Lane?" Elsie asked.

"I don't know much about my flower shop or your bakery, but Lola is having one heck of a day with her parents."

Elsie shook her head. "I can tell by the way you said it you don't mean a swell, good ole time. Lola just needs to roll with it."

I couldn't keep a laugh from shooting out. Elsie's brow lifted. She looked a little hurt.

"Oh, come on, Elsie. Even you have to admit you are not the roll with it type. If you want my honest opinion, I think if you relaxed a little about Les's diet, let him have a few splurges now and then, both of you would be a lot happier. And I think the diet would be more successful." I forged bravely ahead, even beneath her scowl. "There, I've said my piece. You know I love you both, and I just want to help."

Her scowl melted into a sort of resolute frown. "I suppose you're right about that. He's such a stubborn man, but I'm worried about his health."

"I know you are, Elsie. You're a good sister. Just ease up a little. I think Les might get used to the idea of eating healthier."

Just then, over the loudspeaker, Terry announced that there were still free root beer floats.

I clapped Elsie on the shoulder. "And on *that* note, I'm going to step off my advice and healthy eating soapbox and go grab one of those root beer floats. That way I'll have energy to help you carry stuff back to the car."

CHAPTER 10

Terry was auctioning off the sunflower arrangements from the stage. I was pleased to see that people were anxious to win them. They *were* beautiful, and the summer sun had not caused too much wilt yet. On a side table near the stage, there were still about ten root beer floats to choose from. I took an embarrassing amount of time picking one. The most froth and ice cream was a priority. I grabbed my refreshment and stood under some shade to enjoy it. There was a flurry of activity in the park.

Competitors were packing up and portable dog kennels were being broken down into their easier to transport sizes. Avery still wore the stiff look of anger and disappointment as she handed Barrett a crate of grooming supplies to fit into the jigsaw puzzle in the backseat. Barrett, like most men, took his job of packing the space behind the passenger seat seriously, making sure everything fit properly. He also needed to leave room for himself, and he was not a small man. The Cramptons were folding up their portable kennel into flat pieces, while Hamilton and Caprese finished a bowl of food. Everyone looked anxious to leave.

I glanced around for Melody, wondering if she'd ever found

Ellen or if she was still wandering the grounds with Pebbles. I didn't see her anywhere and made the assumption that she found Ellen and went back to her own trailer to pack up for the day.

It was a particularly good root beer float. The paper cup emptied quickly. (In my defense, it was a kid sized cup.) I left my nice spot of shade and headed to a nearby trashcan. As I dropped the cup inside, a scream shot out over the park. People's faces popped up and most stopped what they were doing. Another scream, this one coupled with a panicked cry for help, sent me at a run. Other people followed but with some reluctance at leaving behind their gear and precious pooches. I quickly discovered the source of the scream.

Melody, the groomer, was stumbling in a state of shock, rubbing her hands together and looking frantically around for someone to help her. I reached her first and took hold of her hand.

"What is it?" I asked. "What's wrong? Did you lose Pebbles?"

She was in such a muddle, it took her a second to comprehend my questions. "Pebbles?" she said on a weak breath. "No, it's Ellen." She took a firmer grip of my hand. "Come with me. It's Ellen. I found her in her trailer and—" a muffled sound followed. I couldn't understand what she was saying. She dragged me along the path to Ellen's trailer. Pebbles was sitting stoically inside her pen watching all the excitement around her but not barking or jumping.

"I ripped open the bag," Melody said as we reached the steps. "But I think it's too late."

"The bag? I don't understand."

A crowd gathered around the trailer. It seemed everyone had enough interest to find out what was going on, but no one was concerned enough to follow behind. I wondered briefly if they knew Melody was prone to drama.

We pushed inside the small trailer. It was one of those special custom fifth wheels designed for brief stays at various stops. There was a kitchenette and couch and special pillow with Pebbles' name embroidered on it. Apparently Trigger, with his rustic manners, wasn't allowed to attend elegant events like the dog show.

I stopped just inside the trailer and caught a sneeze before it erupted into a full blown sneeze fit. The lavender smell from Ellen's special shampoo permeated the entire interior. Melody reached for my hand. "She's here. Hurry. I think we need to call an ambulance or something."

I couldn't imagine what she meant by *or something,* but the word *ambulance* sent my adrenaline into overdrive. We stepped around the wall separating the sitting area from the kitchen. Ellen was curled on her side on the ground with a bag over her head. A sparkly dog collar was tightened around her neck holding it in place.

"Oh my gosh," I gasped. I dropped to my knees next to Ellen's very motionless body. "Call for an ambulance and police," I told Melody.

"She looks bad, doesn't she? I ripped open the plastic bag when I found her. Then I ran out to find some help." Melody narrated her harrowing moments as she stood a few feet away from the body on the floor. It seemed the whole thing had traumatized her and rightly so.

"Yes, please make the call."

Melody half stumbled back out of the trailer. I heard a collective gasp as they heard Melody call for an ambulance.

I unfastened the dog collar around Ellen's neck but left it loosely in place. The bag was no longer secured, but it hardly mattered. My few years in medical school had given me enough exposure to dead bodies to know when I was leaning over one. Ellen's eyes were slightly open and lifeless. Her lips were tinged with a faint blue, and there was no breath to move the plastic near her mouth.

Unless Ellen had become so despondent about being called a

cheater, she decided to tie a bag over her head to kill herself, it seemed I was kneeling in the middle of a crime scene. It was the reason I'd decided only to unfasten the collar, an instinctual thing to do when I saw her with a collar tightened around her neck. But I needed to leave the evidence in place.

The poor woman couldn't have been more than forty. Who would have done something like this at a dog show? I studied the thick plastic bag that had been placed over her head. I'd seen it before. The paw prints on the plastic jarred my memory. Avery Hinkle was pulling her champion banner out of a bag just like it the day before. I wasn't certain it was the exact one she was holding, but it sure looked like it. The paw print bag might have been a common item for the competitors. It might have even been Ellen's.

The collar now hanging loosely around her neck looked familiar too. It took less time to jar my memory because I'd been standing right next to a rack of them all day. I was absolutely certain the purple collar with sparkly rhinestones was one of Vivian's creations. Vivian used a certain leather for the collar that had a distinctive leather tanning aroma. I could smell it without leaning closer to the body, even with the pervasive lavender fragrance in the trailer. I wanted to kick myself for not paying more attention to the customers buying up Vivian's sparkly collars. Of course, I never could have predicted that one of them would wind up as part of a gruesome murder plot.

Melody popped her head inside, but it was obvious she'd seen enough of poor Ellen. "The ambulance and police are on their way. And there's a lady out here, the bakery owner. She is wondering if you'll be long. She said something about driving back to Port Danby."

"Tell her I'll be a bit longer."

Melody braved a step into the trailer. She looked close to throwing up. "Is she? You know?"

I didn't want to be the one to start widespread panic and

horror at the dog show, but there wasn't any way to sugarcoat a murder. So I took the coward's way out. "We'll wait for the medical professionals. Tell people outside the trailer that they should clear the area and make room for the emergency vehicles."

"Yes, right away. Poor Pebbles," she muttered as she ducked back out, anxious to carry out her instructions.

I pushed to my feet and peered out the small kitchen window. In the distance, I could see flashing red lights. I knew Briggs was busy on a case, a stake out of sorts, but I wondered if they would call him to the scene of a murder.

I glanced around the trailer. Nothing seemed out of place to indicate any sort of scuffle. I stared down at Ellen, who had just hours before won the dog show. The trophy and ribbon were sitting on the corner of the kitchen counter, waiting to take their places on a display shelf. But now, Ellen would never get to enjoy her trophy or her win. That sad thought led to a logical question. Was Ellen Joyner dead because her dog Pebbles won the Chesterton Dog Show? A second even more obvious question popped into my head. Why on earth didn't she just unbuckle the collar to avoid suffocation? If it wasn't suicide, then it seemed Ellen was unconscious before the killer covered her head in a plastic bag.

CHAPTER 11

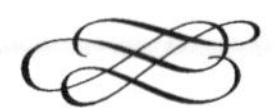

It occurred to me, rather suddenly, that if Detective Briggs didn't arrive with the emergency team, then I wouldn't be involved at the crime scene. After all, I'd had Melody call it in as an emergency, knowing it was not my place to call it a murder. There was a good chance they wouldn't even contact Briggs, especially if he was deep in another case. Briggs usually asked me to sniff out clues with my nose, an effort that was often rewarded when my highly trained nose detected an odor or fragrance that was out of place. The Chesterton Police force might not know that I assisted Detective Briggs on the occasional case. I would certainly be asked to step away from the scene. As the sirens neared, I knew those last few moments might be my only chance to sniff the area.

I dropped back down to my knees, making sure not to come in contact with anything except the vinyl covered floor beneath me. The process of picking out aromatic clues was complicated by the overwhelming scent of lavender and whatever other perfume-laden grooming products permeated the small space. My medical training and general interest in everything science had made me fairly comfortable around dead bodies, but I always found that if I had just seen the person alive and well hours before, the task was more gruesome.

I paused and collected myself before leaning down to Ellen's head, more specifically the hole that Melody had ripped in the bag in a futile attempt to save her life. The bag itself had a strong plastic odor. One I would expect to smell. The pungent smell of sun block mingled with the industrial odor of plastic. The entire dog show had taken place under the hot August sun, so it was easy to conclude that Ellen had slathered on sun block.

I squeezed my eyes shut as I pushed my nose past the hole for a closer sniff. (Ex-med student or not, I was, after all, human.) I hardly needed my hypersensitive nose to detect the all too common at crime scenes metallic odor of blood. I'd been relying on my sense of smell, but it seemed I was going to have to gain enough courage to open my eyes. I was just an inch away from Ellen's dead face as I pried them open.

I scanned her face, her slightly open eyes and limp mouth. As my gaze dropped to the side of her head that was pressed against the floor, I saw the lightest smear of blood. It started near her eyebrow and disappeared beneath her head. It seemed I'd found the answer to my question. Ellen had been knocked unconscious before the killer secured the bag over her head. It was a horrible and macabre plan to kill someone, cause them to suffocate while they were knocked out cold.

The sirens had reached the park. I had just minutes before the crew was led through the crowd to Ellen's trailer at the back of the lot. I moved my nose along Ellen's shirt and found a great deal more lavender. I paused to sneeze. "Excuse me," I said, out of habit. There was no 'bless you' in response. (Thank goodness because that would have been creepy.)

I decided to whisk my nose away and move onto Ellen's hands, a location that often held clues into the last things the victim did before they died. And, if the victim had put up a fight, it occasionally led to the murderer. Although, the scenario in my head of how Ellen died did not show any kind of fight or struggle. Neither did the mostly undisturbed surroundings.

I leaned forward. Before I could lower my nose to the hand resting on the floor nearest me, I caught a distinct scent. "Peanut butter," I muttered to myself. I moved my nose closer to a greasy stain on Ellen's dark blue shirt. It was definitely peanut butter.

I sat back and thought about the entire dog show scandal. It seemed that Avery's accusations were right. Ellen might just have sabotaged Belvedere's showing by feeding him peanut butter. There weren't too many other explanations for someone having peanut butter on their shirt, other than the obvious, a peanut butter and jelly sandwich for lunch.

Voices outside the trailer and footsteps on the stairs let me know help had arrived. Not that there was much help needed. I rose to my feet. The door swung open and a police officer, youngish and slightly nervous looking, entered first. He glanced around to make sure there were no hazards or people waiting in shadows, (not that there were many shadows in the trailer) then waved to someone just outside the door.

The officer stepped aside and let the paramedics pass with their cases of equipment. The first paramedic, a woman with very short hair and glasses was the first to get a glimpse of Ellen.

"Jeez," she gasped and took a step back. Her partner, a man who looked no more than twenty, stepped up next to her. It was a lot of adults and equipment in one cramped space.

"Is she dead?" the young paramedic asked.

"I believe so," I said before the woman could respond.

The medic regained her composure and stepped up next to Ellen. She crouched down next to the body and gently took hold of her wrist. "No pulse."

The officer blanched as he stepped around the kitchenette

counter for the first time. "Jeezus," he said with even more shock than the paramedic. "Looks like someone suffocated her with a bag." It was such an obvious conclusion, I had to turn my head to hide a grin.

The officer grabbed the radio on his shoulder. "This is Officer Burke, we've got an apparent 187. We're going to need a coroner and an evidence team in here stat. Over." He released his radio. "Tuttle and Yates, you two might as well head out. This place is going to get pretty crowded, and there isn't much for you to do," he told the paramedics. "Don't answer any questions from the onlookers. We don't need word about the murder to get out yet," he cautioned them as they left. He turned back and took a more scrutinizing look at me. "Are you a friend, or did you discover the body?"

"Neither actually. A woman named Melody discovered the body. She is a dog groomer. She had been walking the victim's dog around the park. She went looking for the owner to return the dog and found her on the floor. Melody said she ripped open the bag, hoping to help. But you'll want to talk to her to get all the details," I added. "In her distress, Melody came running out of the trailer, looking for someone to help. I followed her in and found the woman on the ground with the bag ripped open. I confess, I instinctively loosened the dog collar that had been fastened around her neck." He started to scowl, so I quickly continued. "In my defense, I didn't know she was dead. It seemed like the first logical thing to do."

Officer Burke took out his notebook. "And your name?" he asked.

"I guess I forgot to mention it. I'm Lacey Pinkerton."

"Pinkerton," he repeated quietly to himself as he wrote it down, then his face popped up. "You're Lacey Pinkerton, the lady with the big nose." He pointed to his own and immediately blushed about his statement. "I don't mean *big* nose, obviously because yours is not big. But I've heard that you can smell the tiniest scent, even if it's mixed in with big scents." He crinkled his nose and sniffed the air. "What is that I'm smelling? Reminds me of my grandmother."

"It's lavender." I could hardly hold back a smile. I'd met many of the Mayfield police officers in various investigations, but this was my first real encounter with Chesterton Police. Port Danby was flanked by two towns, Mayfield, a much bigger, more urban town and Chesterton a sleepy small town that was bordered by farms on one side and expensive beachfront houses on the other. Most of the Mayfield police knew me, especially since I'd started dating Briggs, but it seemed news of my stellar nose had reached west to Chesterton.

Officer Burke seemed a little star struck, which made it even harder for me to refrain from smiling. "Was there anything else you noticed?" he asked. "Anything I might point out to the evidence team?"

I had to admit I was feeling a little full of myself. My expertise was being called upon. I was a long way from that nosy, *nosy* woman who happened upon a dead woman in a pumpkin patch. Back then, Detective Briggs considered me a nuisance (without actually using the word but it showed in his expression). But I'd proved myself and my talent for whiffing out evidence. Now I was an unofficial part of the team.

I cleared my throat in an attempt to sound more important and give weight to my findings. "Yes, I noticed the odor of blood near the victim's head. I believe she has a small wound on the side that is pressed against the floor. I think she might have been struck in the head, knocked unconscious and then suffocated to death with the bag. The victim also has peanut butter on her shirt."

Burke looked less impressed by that finding but then he didn't know anything about the significance of peanut butter during the day's events. But mentioning the shirt reminded me that I hadn't gotten to Ellen's hands.

"If you don't mind, while we're waiting for the coroner, I could run my nose past the victim's hands. Sometimes hands give the most clues. At the very least, they give a picture of what the victim might have been up to before she was killed." My main goal was to check for the incriminating smell of peanut butter. It would help secure the theory that Ellen had indeed sabotaged Avery's chance at winning the trophy.

"Sure but please don't move or touch anything," he said and then looked contrite. "I suppose you already know that."

"Yes, but it's always good to be reminded," I said with a smile.

I knelt back down on the trailer floor and leaned down to run my nose past Ellen's pale, limp hand. It rested on the floor in front of her body.

Officer Burke crouched down nearby and watched with interest. I decided it couldn't hurt to show off a little. After all, I was the famous Lacey Pinkerton with the big nose.

"There is plenty of lavender on her hands, and I'm picking up traces of sun block." I took a deeper whiff. "I can smell grilled onions around her fingertips." I peered up at him. He looked properly impressed, although they were three distinguishable scents that hardly needed hyperactive olfactory cells. I sat back. "I know one of the vendors was selling hamburgers. She might have eaten one for lunch." That erased the notion that she might have had peanut butter and jelly for lunch. Which meant the peanut butter on her shirt came from some other, possibly more nefarious cause. But why couldn't I smell peanut butter on her hand?

I moved cautiously to the other side to run my nose past the hand that had fallen awkwardly behind Ellen when she dropped to the floor. I took a deep breath and smelled the three aforementioned scents, but still no sign of peanut butter.

I sat back. Burke's eyes glittered with intrigue. "Wait till I tell the precinct that I watched Lacey Pinkerton sniff her way around a murder victim."

"Oh, stop," I said coyly but didn't mean it. I was leaning over a murder victim, a terrible tragedy, but I was giddy with pride. "Anyhow, I'm not sure if those scents will lead to anything significant, but there is some peanut butter on her t-shirt and—"

The trailer door opened, and Briggs appeared in the slim doorway. Officer Burke hopped to his feet so fast the trailer shook. "Detective Briggs, I hope it's all right. I let Miss Pinkerton use her nose to sniff out evidence."

Briggs shot me an amused look, then turned his attention back to the officer. "Yes, that's fine, Burke. The coroner van just pulled into the park, so they'll get started in a few minutes." Briggs walked closer. He lowered his hand for me to take and popped me to my feet.

"Miss Pinkerton sure is something," Burke gushed. "I've just been telling her I can't wait to tell everyone at the precinct that I got to work with her."

Briggs shot me a sly smile. "Yes, she is *definitely* something else."

CHAPTER 12

"Burke, why don't you go out and talk to some of the people standing around the scene. They've seen the coroner's van so they know the victim is dead. Find out if anyone saw"—Briggs glanced at his notebook—"Ellen Joyner recently and if anyone saw someone entering this trailer other than Ellen and"—he glanced again at his notebook—"Melody, the woman who discovered the body." It was unusual for him to have to recheck his notes so often. His mind was still preoccupied with the drug case. "I'm going to stick around here to find out what the coroner says about the mark on her head and the time of death."

Officer Burke left to carry out his orders.

Briggs took a brief second to kiss me. "How strange to find Lacey Pinkerton at the scene of a murder."

I bit my lip deciding whether or not to brag. Was it really bragging though? I convinced myself it wasn't. "Apparently, my reputation precedes me, and I'm the toast of the town at the Chesterton Precinct." (Yes, toast of the town might have been taking it a bit too far, but I liked the way it sounded.)

Briggs chuckled, a wonderfully baritone sound. "I'll admit,

your name and your nose do come up occasionally. Although, I have yet to see anyone raise a glass in toast along with it. But, you're definitely the toast of my town. That reminds me"—he shook his head—"I can't keep my thoughts straight these days. Elsie is waiting patiently to hear whether or not she should go back to Port Danby without you. She needs to get back to the bakery."

"That's right. Poor Elsie, I left her standing there forever. I'll go talk to her, then I'll be back."

"You will?" he asked.

I gave him a wide eyed blink. "You can't expect a decent murder investigation to proceed without the famous Lacey Pinkerton and her nose, Samantha. Plus, I've got some insider knowledge I think you'll be interested in hearing."

"I should have guessed. I'll find you after I talk to the coroner. Since you've already done your nasal inspection, we can talk outside. There is hardly enough room in here for Nate to work. Then the evidence team needs space."

"Sounds good." I stepped out of the trailer for the first time since I'd been pulled inside by a highly distraught Melody. Some of the crowd had thinned, mostly to go back to their various places to finish packing. There had been plenty of high drama during the dog show, but the ending had been nothing short of explosive.

Elsie found me before I spotted her in the stragglers and curious onlookers. "Well, Inspector Nose, can we head back to Port Danby? I need to see if Britney managed to get all the work done with her headache."

"I should have just let you go earlier, Elsie. I'm going to stick around here."

She smiled. "I should have know that when I spotted the dreamboat detective walking onto the scene. I'm taking off then. Thanks for your help today."

After talking to Elsie, I was quickly reminded that I, too, owned a shop, and I'd been neglecting it all day. I pulled out my phone to text Ryder.

"How are things going? I was going to stick around at the park for awhile. There's been a murder and I'm assisting." I was tempted to add a smiley face emoji but decided to take the more professional route.

"My boss and the murder scene. They go together like ketchup and fries," he texted back. The man could text with the best of them. A second text came through before I could even think of my response.

"I finished my to-do list and customers are scarce, so Kingston and I are about to sit down to a game of cards."

A laugh shot from my mouth, an inappropriate sound considering that I was standing outside a murder scene. A few of the onlookers arched disapproving brows my direction.

My fingers flew over the keyboard. "Watch that bird. He cheats. P.S. Don't tell him I told you that." It wasn't even all that ludicrous to think about Kingston sitting down to a game of cards. The bird was already under the impression that he was more human than crow.

"I have no problem holding down the fort while you do your thing at the murder scene," Ryder wrote back. "And I'll watch that King doesn't slip any aces under his wing."

"Thanks," I texted back.

I wandered away from the crowd to get a better view of the park. Like Elsie, most of the vendors had left for the day. However, many of the competitors had stuck around, some standing in small circles talking, while others continued cleaning up their spaces. There was a sort of thick cloud of shock, sadness and bewilderment over the park.

Several women had taken Pebbles from her pen. They were walking the dog around the grass. My chest tightened at the sight of the big dog prancing around, seemingly confused that Ellen wasn't on the other end of the leash. And there was Trigger too. He must have been at home, waiting for his mom to come home and feed him. I decided to ask around to find out who might take care of the dogs now.

My answer came before I could even ask. Briggs came out of the trailer with that waxy, expressionless look he wore when some official duty had him feeling grim. "I've just made a call to Ellen's sister. She lives about fifty miles away and is on her way. It seems she's the only family Ellen had left. Their parents are both dead." He took a deep breath. "Worst part of the job."

I pressed my hand against his arm. It wasn't a big show of support, but a long, much needed hug would have been awkward at a crime scene.

We walked away from the clusters of people to a quieter place beneath a tree. "Did the sister have any idea about who might have killed Ellen?"

He shook his head. "Too early to ask that. I didn't want to add to her grief on the phone. We'll interview her once she has gotten over the shock."

"Well then, let me fill you in on some fairly contentious events that took place at the dog show today."

He discretely reached for my hand. "Why was a perfectly perfect florist at a dog show today?"

"I was helping Elsie, of course."

"Then that would lead me to my next question. Why was the town baker at the dog show?"

"Because Britney stayed out too late and she had a headache and Elsie wanted to sell her dog treats. Now, do you want to hear what happened, or are you going to keep on this line of questioning?"

He laughed. "Sorry, yes, tell me what happened."

I motioned toward Pebbles. Some of the other dog owners had gathered around the big dog, hugging and petting her. The dog appeared to enjoy the friendly attention even if she had no idea why she had become the center of their affection.

"Remember that big gray poodle, Pebbles? We saw her with Ellen, the victim, at the beach," I added.

"Yes, I remember."

"She won the show today, only she was not the favorite. The favorite was a cocker spaniel named Belvedere. But there was a little sabotage going on behind the scenes. Belvedere entered the show ring with his snout working hard to finish a sticky bite of peanut butter."

Briggs rubbed his chin. "That's an odd form of sabotage. So someone gave the dog peanut butter to distract him in the show ring?"

"Exactly. You know how dogs get when you give them peanut butter. They love it but it—well, it's not the easiest thing to eat, especially if you're a dog."

Briggs smiled faintly. "Yes, I've been guilty of giving Bear a spoonful or two. It's pretty amusing to watch him eat it."

"It's amusing when you're just playing around but not in the show ring where they expect perfect obedience. The judge wasn't able to get a good look at Belvedere's conformation, so the ribbon went to Pebbles. Up until this year, the poodle was always the runner up. Apparently, Ellen had been coveting that first place ribbon for some time. The peanut butter mishap allowed her dream to come true. I was at the show and things got pretty heated. Avery Hinkle, the woman who owns Belvedere, accused Ellen of sabotage right in front of the entire crowd. Ellen was still on stage with Pebbles, enjoying her moment of glory, when Avery started yelling at her, calling her a cheater and a saboteur. Ellen left the stage in tears. That's the last time I saw her alive."

Briggs had pulled out his notebook and was writing down the details. "Did you say her name was Avery Hinkle?" he asked.

"Yes, and she might have been right about Ellen. I smelled

peanut butter on Ellen's shirt. It wasn't on her hands but then the lavender grooming products were sort of overwhelming in that trailer. Remember, Ellen owned a dog grooming supply business. Her lavender shampoo is very popular."

"That's right. She gave us her business card. I think it's still in the pocket of my shorts."

"There's one more thing," I said. "It might be important."

Briggs nodded. "Go ahead."

"Yesterday, I came here to the park to deliver the sunflower arrangements. Most of the competitors were just setting up. I happened to notice Avery Hinkle because she was pulling out a banner about Belvedere being last year's champion. The banner was inside a thick plastic bag dotted with paw prints."

Comprehension crossed Briggs' face. "Like the one pulled over the victim's head?"

"Exactly."

He wrote down that detail. "Seems like my unofficial partner has already done a lot of leg work—and nose work—on this one." He winked at me. "Let's find out if the officers on the scene have done as well as you. Although, I'm not counting on it."

CHAPTER 13

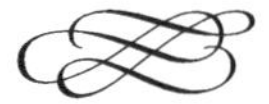

Officer Burke caught up to us after he'd interviewed a few of the bystanders. Most of them were competitors, and they were quick to relay exactly what I'd told Briggs about the sabotage incident and the accusations that flew afterward.

Burke seemed a little flustered about having to report back to Detective Briggs. Apparently, the Chesterton Police weren't used to having a murder in their town. Burke shuffled through his notepad and cleared his throat. "Sir," he addressed Briggs formally, "aside from many witnesses mentioning the incident at the dog show, several people claimed that Miss Hinkle had been lurking around the deceased woman's trailer. I decided to ask Avery Hinkle where she was for the past few hours." He looked up hesitantly. "I couldn't narrow down the time span since we don't have time of death yet from the coroner," he added.

"That's fine, Burke," Briggs said. "What did you find out?"

Burke perused his notes. "Miss Hinkle claimed she was busy packing up her belongings so she could leave the park." He cleared his throat again. "I took the liberty of asking her to remain on the grounds for awhile longer. I thought you might want to have a word with her."

Briggs nodded. "That's good, Burke. Thank you. It's always hard to secure a murder scene when there are droves of people milling about. Did you ask her specifically about why she was near Miss Joyner's trailer? Did she have a reasonable purpose for being there?"

Burke returned to his notes. "Yes, and I corroborated her story with another person. Miss Hinkle said she was looking for her dog. Apparently, a Miss Melody Langley, is a hired dog walker. Miss Hinkle had paid Miss Langley to walk her dog"—he looked at his notes again—"her dog Belvedere while she packed up her belongings. She went looking for the dog walker and Belvedere. She happened to find them in the grassy area behind Miss Joyner's trailer. Miss Langley said that is exactly what happened. Although, she said she handed off the leash to Miss Hinkle and left them standing in that grassy area while the dog finished his—" another throat clearing, "finished his business."

Briggs pulled out his own notebook. It was a rather quaint, cute meeting of the pen and notepad set. He wrote a few things down that made Burke beam. He was pleased to have found crucial information for the head detective.

"So the dog walker, Miss Langley, handed off the leash and left Miss Hinkle and her dog alone in the grassy area behind the victim's trailer. Did you find anyone else who might have see Miss Hinkle after that?"

His earlier proud grin vanished and Burke's face fell. "Sorry, sir, I didn't establish her whereabouts after that."

"That's all right, Officer Burke. I'm planning to talk to Miss Hinkle myself. I'll ask her about it. Why don't you find out how far along the coroner is with his examination." He continued on with some other instructions, so I stepped away to read a text that'd beeped through earlier.

"I'm freaking out, boss," Ryder wrote. "Lola and I are going to dinner with her parents tonight. This will be our first official introduction. What if they hate me?"

I wrote quickly back, upset that I'd taken so long to check my messages. It was obvious Ryder needed my support. "You are literally impossible to hate so take that notion out of your head. I'll be back in Port Danby soon so you can take off for the day. Maybe you should go to the gym and work out or take a bike ride to get rid of some of the anxiety you're feeling."

"That's a great suggestion. I'll see you when you get here."

I returned to Briggs. He had just finished with Burke. "I'm going to walk over and talk to Avery Hinkle. If you're interested, you can tag along."

I laughed dryly. "When have you known me to not be interested in a suspect interview? Is she a suspect or am I jumping the gun? It seems like she should be."

"Not a suspect yet but definitely a person of interest. I want to ask her about the bag that was found over the victim's head. Something I would never have known about without my great partner." He reached around my waist and gave me a fleeting squeeze.

Avery Hinkle seemed ready to leave. Her boyfriend, Barrett, was leaning against the side of the truck looking at his phone, while Avery was walking Belvedere around a nearby patch of grass for a last order of *business* before climbing into the truck.

Briggs leaned his head closer as we walked toward the couple. "Is the tall guy next to the truck, Mr. Hinkle?" he asked from the side of his mouth.

"Boyfriend, I think. He did try and stop her from making a big scene during the show, but she wasn't in the mood to be stopped."

"Miss Hinkle?" Briggs called.

Avery looked up from her dog. "Yes?" She looked perplexed and slightly annoyed. "If you're with the police, I've already been interviewed." Her mouth pulled into a tight frown. "Not sure how I've become the center of this investigation. The incident at the dog show left me angry, but I certainly wouldn't murder Ellen over a trophy, for heaven's sake." She was off on a confessional and rant before Briggs even got in one word or showed her his badge. "There are just too many gossip-prone people in this show circuit," she added. It seemed she had soured on her fan base since the murder. "I'd like to go home now if that's all right with the police."

Briggs pulled out his badge. "Yes, just a few questions, then you can go." Barrett was watching the scene, but he didn't seem inclined to come over and support his girlfriend, even though she was clearly irritated. That might have even been the reason he decided to stay clear.

Avery glanced at the badge. "Detective Briggs, yes, of course, I've heard of you." Her questioning gaze flicked my direction.

"Miss Pinkerton is assisting me on the case," he said curtly, letting her know that was his full explanation whether she liked it or not.

"I thought she was the baker's assistant. I saw her selling dog treats a few hours ago." There was just enough snip in her tone to make me stiffen. But I kept my cool, mostly because I wanted to stick around for the questions, and I was always giddy with pride when Briggs introduced me as his assistant.

"She is a woman that wears many hats," Briggs said briskly. "Miss Hinkle, I understand you were seen near the victim's trailer before the body was discovered."

"Yes, as I explained to the officer, I walked over there to find Belvedere." She motioned down to her dog, who had sat down on his haunches to rest after the long day. "Melody, the dog groomer, was walking him for me while I packed the truck. I happened to find her on the grass behind the trailer."

"What did you do after Miss Langley handed off the leash?"

She was visibly flustered. It had been a long and unhappy day for Avery Hinkle. She seemed ready to crumple into a pile of sobs.

"Well, if you know anything about dogs, Detective Briggs," she said sharply, but with a slight waver, "you let them finish what they need to do. Just like now, since we're not at home, where Belvedere has the freedom to go out into the yard through his dog door, I walk him around until he is finished relieving himself. I was told I needed to wait in the park, but I'll be honest, I'm really ready to go home and put this disastrous dog show behind me."

"I understand," Briggs said in his most sympathetic tone. "Just one other question. We've retrieved a piece of evidence from the crime scene that we have reason to believe belongs to you."

Avery's cheeks drained of color. She looked as if someone had just socked her in the stomach. "I don't understand. What piece of evidence?"

"A thick plastic bag with paw prints was found at the crime scene." I knew Briggs didn't want to give away any clues about how Ellen was murdered. Although, I found it hard to believe that Melody hadn't already conveyed all the grim details to everyone.

"So it's true? Someone tied a plastic bag around Ellen's head?" she asked, confirming my prediction about Melody. "I don't know anything about—" She stopped and more color drained from her face.

"Miss Hinkle?" Briggs asked. "Are you all right?"

"My bag," she said weakly, then collected herself. "It's been packed in the truck now but I arrived with a large banner mentioning that Belvedere was the 2018 Chesterton Champion. I had it stored in a thick plastic bag with paw prints on the plastic."

"Could you show me that banner and bag right now?" Briggs asked.

"No," she said. "I mean, I would only someone stole the bag. I ended up using a paper bag for the banner. I searched all over for the plastic one but I couldn't find it." She covered her mouth to stifle a gasp. "The person who killed Ellen must have stolen it from my belongings. I can't believe it. Who would do such a thing?"

Briggs wrote down Avery's account of the stolen bag. "I'll let you go then, Miss Hinkle. Officer Burke has your contact information in case we need to talk to you again."

She nodded but didn't say anything else. She looked genuinely shaken at the prospect that someone stole her plastic bag to kill Ellen Joyner.

Briggs and I walked away.

"She has the most motive and there's a key piece of evidence connecting her to the murder, but Avery Hinkle doesn't act as if she just killed someone," I said.

"She was pretty defensive at first," Briggs reminded me. "But her shock does seem pretty authentic. I need to talk to the coroner and the evidence team. I take it you need a ride back to Port Danby?"

"That would be nice. Ryder is in a bit of a state because he has to go to dinner with Lola and her parents."

Briggs shook his head. "Ah, yes, the meet the parents dinner. Every boyfriend's worst nightmare."

"What do you mean? My parents loved you. My mom asks me if I'm still dating James every time we talk. In fact, she asks that before she even asks how I'm doing. I could be sinking in a hole of quicksand and just calling to tell her goodbye, but she'd miss my fond farewell because she'd be jumping right into her question about our relationship."

"Where are you hanging out lately that you might get mired in quicksand?" he asked with a laugh. "I'll find an officer to give you a ride back. I've got to stick around for a bit longer to see if anything important comes up."

"All right, just don't find anything too important without me."

CHAPTER 14

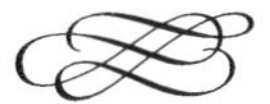

I felt sorry for Ryder as he left the shop. He looked wound as tight as a rubber band. He had decided a run on the beach might be the best way to unwind and I agreed. I checked my phone several times as I plucked away at my keyboard typing out purchase orders. There was no word from Briggs, but I was sure he'd fill me in once he learned anything significant.

The bell on the door rang and Elsie's 'yoo hoo' followed. I headed out to the storefront. She was holding a pink box. "Just wanted to bring you a little thank you gift for helping me out at the park."

"You didn't need to do that." I took the box from her hands and set it on the counter to open it. It was filled with multicolored French macarons. "They smell delicious and almond-y." I lifted out a pale green one that had the fragrant aroma of pistachio. "Hmm," I moaned as I took a bite of the delicate meringue. "So worth standing in a hot park all day."

Elsie pulled a peanut butter dog treat out of her pocket. The move sent Kingston into one of his ice skating dances across his perch. Elsie walked over and dropped it in his bowl, then hopped up on a stool at the island. "I sent Britney home to get some sleep. She got everything done today on the work list, but by the time I got back to the bakery, she was wandering around like a zombie, unable to focus. That Dash," she muttered. She always had to add in a negative comment about my neighbor. I felt sort of bad for Dash. At the same time, I wanted to give him a good shake. He knew Elsie was watching his every move, yet he didn't seem to change his habits.

"Did they find out who killed the dog owner?" Elsie picked at some of the leaf debris on the counter. "I'm sure it was that woman who lost. While I was standing outside the trailer waiting for Inspector Nosey to finish her work"—she looked pointedly at me—"I heard everyone gossiping and theorizing that last year's champion was raging mad because someone fed her dog peanut butter and that caused her to lose the show."

"She does seem like the obvious choice for suspect. The competitors, at least the top people, do seem to take the show very seriously. However, it's a big stretch to think the sore loser would resort to murder, even if there was sabotage involved. But then, people have killed for less."

Elsie tapped the counter and was off to the next topic. Especially since murder mysteries held little interest for the woman. "I've been making a list of possible desserts I can make that are vegan. I know dates can make a delicious caramel, and I was researching it a bit and found that you can make a good egg substitute with ground flax seed. There are various kinds of nut butters that act as a substitute for butter."

"You're really getting into this vegan thing." It was getting late so I decided to start cleaning up for the day. I grabbed a sponge from the potting area and returned to the work island to wipe it down. "Won't it be a big extra cost to add all these new ingredients to your stockroom? Dates aren't cheap, and I tried almond butter once." I temporarily stopped my task. "Delicious, by the way. Very rich and decadent. But I think the small jar cost me eight dollars."

"Yes, it's true. I'll probably have to charge more for the vegan treats, but I do occasionally get a customer asking for something vegan. Then there's my brother who is walking around with butter and confectioner's sugar pumping though his veins."

"Poor Les, did he eat his vegetables today?" I asked as I swept leaf and stem remnants into my hand.

"I doubt it. I fixed him a perfectly delicious lunch with a whole wheat hummus and vegetable wrap, but since I wasn't around, he probably tossed it and walked down to Franki's Diner for a greasy bacon burger and chili fries. I think he's craving bad food even more now because he knows I want him to change his diet."

I paused and tilted my head at her. "Then try my plan and give him some leeway. You just said it yourself, he's being more defiant because you are forcing him to change."

She waved her hand. "I'm not forcing him. He's a grown man, after all."

My head tilt remained, but I added an eyebrow lift.

"All right, so I'm forcing him a bit. It's for his own good. And yes, maybe your idea is the way to go. I'll let him have his fun on the weekend. After all, how much damage can he do in two days? Never mind. Don't answer that. I've seen him plow through a plate of nachos in minutes." She slapped the counter again. "Well, I've got to finish cleaning up. Enjoy the macarons."

"Oh, I plan to. Thanks again."

CHAPTER 15

I was shutting down my office computer when the bell rang. "Darn it. Forgot to put up the closed sign and lock the door." I headed out to greet the customer, hoping they just needed a quick bouquet or card. Much to my pleasure, I discovered my wonderful boyfriend standing in the shop. He was snooping in the pink bakery box and dropped the lid like a kid caught with his hand in the cookie jar.

A laugh spurted from my mouth. "Guilt is not a good look for you, my friend. Which is odd because just about every other emotion looks marvelous on that handsome face." I pressed up against him and gave him a kiss. "You may have a macaron. Just not the lemon or the pistachio. Those are my favorite, and I *did* stand in the hot sun all day to earn them."

Briggs opened the lid on the box again. "I'm not fluent in macaron. Which ones are pistachio and lemon?"

"Yellow and green," I said as I walked to the door to flip over the closed sign.

"That makes sense." He reached in and pulled out a caramel confection. "Thought I might miss you. You're closing up late."

"Not really. I've been in the office doing paperwork. I just forgot to flip the sign and lock the door."

He frantically lifted his palm under his chin to catch the flaky bits of almond meringue. "Good but messy." He brushed some of the white residue off his shirt. "Guess it wouldn't be too professional or manly to show up to a stake out with crumbs of meringue on my shirt."

My shoulders sank. "You have to work tonight? But it's Saturday."

"Well aware of that, but, unfortunately, criminals don't calendar in weekends. In fact, there's been an increase in activity, so we're expecting a delivery any time. I've got to relieve one of the team members."

"So on top of having nothing to do, I have to spend those long, lonely hours worrying about you," I said.

"There's an easy solution to that. Don't worry." He walked across the room to give Kingston a head rub. "You're reading too much into this job."

I harrumphed. "That's because I can see the stress of it in your face. That's rare with my cool, calm and collected man."

"I'm still that man, just tired from waiting these guys out." He walked toward me and brushed his finger along my cheek, a gesture that always put me off my guard and made me feel a little tipsy. "I'm sure it's going to end soon, but I'll probably be on duty all weekend. What will you do tonight without me?" He lowered his hand.

I shrugged. "Oh, I don't know. Guess I'll have to go through my contact list and see if any of my other boyfriends are available."

His crooked smile appeared. "Funny girl."

I wrapped my arm around his. "I guess I'll skip the contact list and sit at home with my bird, my cat and my macarons. I've been meaning to get back to the Hawksworth murders anyhow. I need to look at my notes, see what I have and figure out where to go next." I released his arm to finish closing up for the night. "Speaking of murders—" I grabbed the broom for one more quick sweep. "Did they find anything else at the scene?"

"Like you theorized, the victim had been hit on the head and knocked unconscious. It was a good blow according to Nate, but he doesn't think it was enough to kill her. That's when the killer turned to plan B and suffocated her while she was out cold. Officer Burke did a search of nearby trashcans and recovered what we think was used to hit her on the head. It was a metal stake like the kind that was jammed in the grass to hold onto dog leashes. There was blood on the stake, so it's heading to the lab for testing. We aren't holding out too much hope for clear fingerprints because the stake was rusty and was probably held in someone's palm, which would cause prints to smear. But you never know."

"And suspects?" I asked.

Briggs shrugged. "I'm not sure. The Chesterton Police are going to take the lead on this one, at least until I finish with this drug bust. So far, the Hinkle woman is at the top of the list because she was seen in the area and she had apparent motive."

"And her plastic bag was used for the suffocation," I added. I rested the broom against the wall and leaned over to pick up the dustpan. "Although," I said as I popped back, "that Avery Hinkle doesn't strike me as dumb. Would she be careless enough to leave the bag on the victim? Of course, I don't know her that well. Maybe she's sillier than her exterior lets on."

Briggs got a text. He checked his phone. "I've got to go." He walked over, took hold of both my arms and brought my face up to his for a nice kiss. "I'll see you later and keep away from those other boyfriends. You're mine, all mine."

I smiled. "I kind of like the sound of that. Be careful and keep an eye out for bad guys, please."

"I intend to."

I blew him a kiss as he looked back from the door.

CHAPTER 16

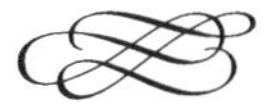

Some of Elsie's new health plan had started to seep its way into my eating habits. It was a slow seep, of course, as evidenced by the root beer float, caramel cookies and the five, yes five macarons I'd had since Elsie walked into the store with the pink box. If I thought about it, I could technically blame my last three sugary indiscretions on Elsie. Still, the mad bakery woman was the inspiration behind my nutritious dinner salad, complete with artichoke hearts, broccoli and garbanzo beans. I gobbled down every last bite, then set to work reading through my notes on the Hawksworth murders.

It all started on a terrible night, in the massive Victorian home at the top of Maple Hill. The site was now a historical landmark and one of Port Danby's main attractions, other than a lovely beach and Pickford Lighthouse. On that fateful night of October 7, 1906, the entire Hawksworth family, a prominent and rich family in the community, were murdered as they relaxed for the evening. Bertram and Jill Hawksworth were murdered alongside their three children, Phoebe, William and Cynthia all between the ages of ten and fifteen. The police at that time closed the case quickly as a murder-suicide. The murder weapon was found in Bertram's right hand. Even though the first investigator at the scene, Officer Gilly, had seemed to question the theory that Bertram shot his family before turning the gun on himself, Gilly was transferred mid-case to another precinct and the tragic event was closed. The town went on believing the worst of Mr. Hawksworth, that he had, in cold blood, shot dead his entire family, children included, before taking his own life.

My own investigation into the hundred-year-old case had led me up the hill to the Hawksworth Manor. The vast site included a gardener's shed where the town had displayed a few rather uninspiring artifacts left behind by the family. Gruesome pictures of the crime had given me my first real break in the case. One photo in particular, one that showed Bertram on the floor, in his own blood, gripping the gun in his right hand, helped to nail down my own theory that Bertram was not the culprit but rather the victim. While perusing original Port Danby newspapers, I'd found a picture of Bertram Hawksworth signing the documents for his future shipyard. It was to be built right alongside Port Danby's shoreline. He was holding the pen in his left hand. As little as I knew about shooting a gun, I was certain if you were left-handed, you would shoot with the left. It seemed easy to deduce that someone had place the gun in Bertram's right hand after killing him. Only that someone hadn't considered the possibility that Bertram was left-handed. It was exactly that, which had given Officer Gilly pause on the case. But he had been whisked away so quickly, he was never able to follow up on it. Oddly enough, there seemed to be no reason for his sudden transfer. The left handedness issue had spurred on my curiosity. Since then, whenever I had a few spare moments, I did some investigating.

I browsed through my haphazard notes, reminding myself what each cryptic statement meant and what it had to do with the case. *Harvard Price abruptly ends the Hawksworth shipyard project.* I wasn't sure how it was connected to the murder, but it was, no doubt, a blow to Bertram Hawksworth. He had plans to go on with the lucrative, industrious project until Mayor Harvard Price put an end to it. The Price family had been in the Port Danby mayor's seat for over a hundred years, including today. Harvard's great grandson, Harlan Price, was the current mayor of the town, and he had, for some reason, taken an instant disliking to me. He wasn't too fond of my pet crow either but that was fine. The rest of the town adored Kingston. *Front page picture of Harvard Price.* It was another cliff note I'd made about my research through old newspapers. It was taken the day that Mayor Price halted the shipyard project. Mayor Price's daughter, from his first marriage, Jane Price, was standing in the picture holding the Port Danby account ledger. Further research showed that Jane had been town treasurer for a few years before she was sent away. I couldn't find the reason for her leaving town. When I approached the current Mayor Price about his Great Aunt Jane he became irate and stormed away angry.

Who is in the unmarked grave? A nagging mystery about the Hawksworth family that so far had not been solved, revolved around an unmarked grave in the Hawksworth family plot in the town's church cemetery. An old picture showed that the unmarked grave, an unusually small plot, had been filled before the family was murdered. I'd toyed with the notion that it had been the grave of a beloved hunting dog or some such animal, but it seemed strange to have it buried in a church graveyard. Not to mention, if it had been so beloved as to earn a spot in the family plot, then wouldn't it also have been important enough to earn a gravestone, or, at the very least, a plaque. I hadn't been able to find any information on who might be buried in the grave.

Hawksworth account ledger signed off by Jane Price. Lola's knowledge of antiques helped lead me to the hidden key on an unlocked trunk that was part of the display in the makeshift museum set up in the Hawksworth garden shed. The trunk contained men's clothing items. I could only assume they had belonged to Bertram. I also discovered an account ledger that had been signed off by Jane Price, which meant she was not only town treasurer but an accountant for the Hawksworth family.

Love letters with lavender. The same trunk contained a few informal love letters written to *Teddy* from *Button.* A sprig of lavender, ancient and dried but still intact, was tucked into the letters. I could only assume they were from Jill to Bertram, either that or Bertram had a mistress. The latter sounded much more intriguing and plausible. I'd discovered with more research that Jill and Bertram had been part of an arranged marriage. Their wedding day photo in the paper did not exactly show an overjoyed couple.

The mayor has a different ledger. My research at the wonderful Chesterton Library and their microfiche machines, helpful technological relics that came in handy for glancing through old newspapers without worrying about ripping a brittle page or making sure it folded neatly back up. The microfiche helped me scan a number of front page headlines, but one that stood out to me the most wasn't about the headline but more about the grainy photo. It was only a small, inconsistent detail, but my intuition kept poking at me, letting me know that it was significant. I just wasn't sure how. I had first seen the Port Danby town ledger in the picture with Jane Price. A paper dated a year later showed Mayor Price sitting at his desk behind an ornate silver inkwell and the town ledger. It was embossed leather with the town's name, just like the one Jane Price had been holding in the earlier picture. Only in the later picture, the ledger had silver corners. It was a different ledger altogether. There was always the possibility that a new, fancy ledger had been purchased, but my detective's instinct told me something was off.

I stared down at my notes. There was a lot there and at the

same time there wasn't much. At least not anything that would point out the murderer and say 'ah ha, you are guilty'.

I got up from the table and carried in my cup of tea and the empty salad bowl. Nevermore had curled up on the couch for his fiftieth nap of the day. Kingston had finished his dinner and folded his beak under his wing to sleep.

The late summer sun was starting to set, but there was still just enough daylight for a trip up Maple Hill to the Hawksworth Manor. I was bored and it was Saturday night. No better way to spend it than sitting in the dank, dusty gardener's shed combing through the old trunk. Fortunately for this detective, a rebellious teen back from Briggs' day in high school had broken the lock on the gardener's shed. He'd left it so that it looked locked, but the open side of the padlock did not engage, leaving it permanently unlocked.

The Hawksworth property was dark and creepy, and the house was one bad storm from crumbling into a heap, but the town teens loved to hang out there. After living just a block down from Maple Hill for a few years, I knew the teens didn't travel up there until after dark. What was the fun of visiting a haunted house in daylight? Since I was more than a bit terrified of the dark, I was just as happy to travel up to the house while the sun was still smiling.

With any luck, I'd find a new clue and something to add to my pile of scribbles and notes.

CHAPTER 17

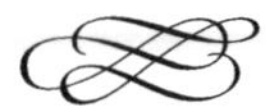

Dusk had lowered its pinkish curtain on me before I'd even reached the top of Maple Hill. I needed to hurry before I lost the daylight altogether. Since my decision to hike up to the Hawksworth Manor had been last second, my only preparation for the evidence collecting adventure had been to put on sandals and pull on a light sweater. It was still warm outside, but once the sun was down, the ocean breeze could get chilly.

I reached the vast lot that had once been the Hawksworth estate. It had, by far, the best ocean view in the entire town. The looming, dilapidated Victorian house looked older and more lonely every time I saw it. There were less dusty window panes and more pieces of plywood to cover the openings. A rather incongruous chain link fence had been constructed around the entire structure to keep people from sneaking inside. It wasn't much of a deterrent for a spritely teenager, or a curious twenty-something like myself. I had actually snuck in once and quickly found myself trapped on the inside by a broken door handle. My neighbor Dash had come to my rescue that damp, foggy morning. I hadn't stepped foot inside since. My short, scary tour of the home assured me that there was nothing stable about the ceiling, walls or stairs. The town kept the unsafe structure around for the visitors and curious tourists. People who visited the somewhat lackluster museum set up in the gardener's shed liked to finish their tour by strolling around the exterior of the house, a house that was, of course, rumored to be teeming with the ghosts of the Hawksworth family.

I headed past the manor to the gardener's shed at the side of the property. With August slowly turning into a new school year, the largest swarm of visitors and tourists had already passed through Port Danby and its historical point of interest. A month ago, I probably would have run into people just heading back down to the town, but this evening, I was completely alone. The teens wouldn't be up at the site until dark. I had a good chunk of time where I had the place to myself. The only thing not on my side was the waning sunlight.

I hurried to the door of the shed. A spark of concern hit me when I considered that after all these years the city might have fixed the lock. I gave it a yank, and sure enough, it dropped open. In truth, there wasn't much inside of any value, except the intrinsic value the town placed on its *museum* pieces.

Even though many people had traipsed around the small interior in the past few months, it smelled dark and dusty inside. I startled at the taxidermy stuffed black crow sitting on the top shelf staring down at me with its black glass eyes. I'd expected the creepy thing, but it still always made me step back. It wasn't as if I'd never had a big black bird scowling down at me before. And right in my own kitchen.

I crouched down next to my main point of interest, Bertram Hawksworth's trunk. No one else knew what was inside of it. I'd discovered, much to my chagrin, that no one had ever taken the time to try and open it. I'd been told they wanted to preserve the lock on the trunk, and since there had presumably been no key, they'd left the lock untouched. But Lola, who knew a great deal about old trunks and boxes, told me that often a key was hidden in a compartment under the trunk. That was exactly where I found the hidden key. Naturally, I'd kept the secret to myself. A good investigator never gave away her sources and methods . . . or her secret keys.

Sand and grit pressed into my bare knees as I knelt and then leaned down to retrieve the key from its secret compartment. On my trek up the hill, I'd decided that I would go back to the account ledgers. I wasn't sure why or if it would bear any fruit but something about the account books intrigued me.

I turned my head to sneeze away the century old dust that floated up from the decaying straw boaters and ascots. I pushed aside the three brittle letters that Button had written to Teddy and pulled out the second and last ledger that held the accounts of Bertram Hawksworth up to his death in 1906.

The leather binding creaked as I opened the ledger. A man named Moore had signed off as the accountant in 1900, the first year in the ledger. Then Jane Price had apparently taken over the books. She signed off on the accounts for about a year. Since she left town the next year, it made sense that a different accountant took over after that. The third bookkeeper's signature was too hard to decipher.

The light coming through the half open doorway was getting weaker by the minute. I pushed to my feet and carried the book outside to a small bench where visitors waited when the shed was filled to capacity. I opened the book further toward the back, wanting to get closer to Bertram's year of death. I ran my fingers down the columns. There were payments to creditors, city tax fees, tailors and dressmakers. The person who kept the books wrote down every name and even the address of each entry, along with the amount paid or received. By all indications, Bertram had a lot of money going out but not a lot coming in. He seemed to have been one of those typical wealthy Victorians whose bank account had been mostly built by inheritance and family money. The shipyard seemed to have been an ambitious attempt to increase the family fortune with an enterprise he could call his own and pass down to his children. Only that attempt was squashed by the town mayor.

My finger passed over a strange entry that just read *gift*. There was no name of business or address or anything that could allow an auditor to know where the money went. It was a very specific sum of seventy-three dollars. Not a small amount for that time period.

I flipped through, looking to see if there were any other 'gift' entries. A few pages over, I was at the next month, June 1903. I scrolled down and found the same entry. Gift was in the paid to column and the amount gifted was seventy-three dollars. Even though I was never a bookkeeper, it seemed someone had something to hide. Otherwise, at the very least, there would have been a footnote like birthday or anniversary. Only those were annual events, not monthly. I turned to July and ran my finger down the column. Another gift of seventy-three dollars. I flipped a few pages more and quickly found that Bertram Hawksworth was gifting someone seventy-three dollars on the tenth of every month.

Laughter drifted up from below, signaling that teens were about to swarm the place. I needed to lock up the trunk and, with any luck, be half way down the hill before they arrived. I didn't want to spoil their fun. I also wanted to avoid some loose lipped teen asking why an *old* person was hanging around the place.

As I hopped up from the bench, a piece of paper fell halfway out of the ledger. I stopped and opened to the back of the book where the piece of paper had slipped from its hiding spot, between the leather cover and the paper binding. I yanked it the rest of the way out and opened the handwritten note.

"If I am dead, raven knows all. B. H."

Reading it several times didn't get me any closer to the meaning. There was no question that Bertram Hawksworth had written the note, but I had no idea what it meant. I pushed the slip of paper back into its hiding place. It seemed my jaunt up the hill had been worth it. If nothing else, I had a few more interesting facts to jot down on my scrambled notes about the Hawksworth murders.

But Bertram and Jill would have to wait now because there was a new murder in town. I was certain it required my expertise. And I had a few ideas on where to start.

CHAPTER 18

Lola rushed into the shop as I finished trimming the last of a dozen roses. She leaned against the front wall, out of view of the door and window. "What a long weekend. Thought it would never end. I'm going to have to hide in here. My alien abduction plan never came to fruition. Stupid aliens. Where are they when you need them?"

Ryder popped his head up from the potting bench. He shook his head but didn't say anything, which was probably a good decision. Unfortunately, Lola caught the slight head shake. She left her wall and half-skipped across the floor.

"If you think they are so wonderful, then maybe you should adopt them as your family."

"Uh oh," I muttered to the lustrous red roses in front of me. Ryder had mentioned that the dinner out was fine and that he got along very well with both Cynthia and John. I hadn't dug out many more details, deciding all had gone well and the tension was over. I hadn't considered the possibility that the night hadn't gone as smoothly for Lola as it had for Ryder.

"I already have a set of parental units, thank you very much."

Ryder put the pot he was holding down on the counter. "Look, I thought they were both being pretty cool last night. Your dad and I got along great, and your mom was fun. She has a good personality like her daughter." He winked sweetly, but I knew Ryder was too far in to dig himself out with a compliment and a wink.

"Oh yes, my mom is fun," Lola said darkly. "So fun. Very, very fun. She is so fun that she is at this very moment going through all the shop receipts from the past twelve months to make sure I was calculating the tax correctly." A harsh laugh followed. "I mean, have you ever heard of anything so darn fun?"

Ryder looked up at the ceiling. "You're right. Where are those darn aliens when you need them?"

I swept out from behind the counter to come to my faithful employee's rescue. "Lola, I've got to head over to Chesterton. I want to check out a dog boutique. I'll buy you an ice cream, double scoop."

Lola seemed to be considering my offer. I was certain the double scoop had pushed her over the fence to the yes side. "I suppose a double scoop of rocky road might make me forget that my boyfriend has now sided with my *fun* mom."

"Come on, Lo-lo, you're not being fair," Ryder said.

I tried to flick a little head shake his direction to let him know an ice cream and an hour away would probably wipe away her mood, but he didn't catch my hint.

He walked toward her. "Would you have preferred it if they hated me? Maybe I should have acted like a jerk and tossed food around the table and cussed. I was worried about them hating me. I was relieved that they seemed to like me. But you—" he shook his head. "Never mind. There's no winning with you."

I couldn't blame Ryder, but I wished he had quit at the 'you're not being fair' statement.

Lola swept around and looked at me. Her mouth was pulled tight in anger. "Are we going for that ice cream or what?"

"I'll get my purse." I headed down the hallway. "Gee, this should be the best ice cream trip ever."

There was a frosty patch of silence for the first leg of our journey. My car puttered along Culpepper Road and onto Highway 48, the road leading to Chesterton. Lola leaned forward and messed with the radio until she finally landed on something that suited her mood, a heavy metal tune that was either terrible or I was getting too old to appreciate the clamor. But I decided not to complain. My friend obviously needed to cool off, and if heavy metal was good therapy, then who was I to stop it.

After the discordant song ended, I glanced over at Lola. "Do you want to talk about it?" I asked, not knowing if I was even in the mood to listen but putting the offer out there anyhow.

"Nope." She adjusted her cap. I noticed that since her mom had complimented her hair and made note of Lola being without a hat, my best friend had been donning every hat in her wardrobe, the more tattered the better.

She fussed with the radio a few minutes and then turned it off in disgust when she couldn't find anything she liked. "Why are we going to a dog boutique when your only pets are a cat and bird?"

I was relieved she broke her stony silence. A different topic would help ease her mood. "The murder victim at the dog show had been suffocated with a plastic bag. The killer tied the bag around her neck with a fancy dog collar."

Lola crinkled her nose. "That is as creepy as it is sort of cool. I mean who uses fancy dog collars for murder? Someone who is either sick or an independent thinker."

"Well, so much for me hoping the new topic would get you out of your dark mood." I turned onto the street where Viv's Dog Boutique was located.

"You're the one who chose murder as your topic to lighten my mood." She rolled down the window and put her hand out. "I think it's hotter in Chesterton than in Port Danby. I guess they don't get the ocean breeze as much."

I found a parking spot a block away from Vivian's shop. I turned off the motor. I knew I was getting myself into a sticky mess, but I decided to let my friend know where I came down on the whole last few minutes in the shop. "You know Ryder is right. He was so nervous that your parents wouldn't like him—"

"Everyone likes him. I don't know why he was worried." She opened the car door. "I just wish my parents would like *me*." She shut the door and headed to the sidewalk.

I climbed out and raced to catch up to her. "You don't seriously believe that your parents don't like you?"

"Well, I guess my dad doesn't seem to *dislike* me, but my mom finds fault with everything I do. I'm surprised she hasn't come up with a way to criticize the way I breathe. I think that's the only thing left on the table."

I laughed.

Lola looked at me. "Thanks for all your support, chum."

"I had to laugh because my mom hasn't even left *that* one on the table. She thinks I move my shoulders too much when I breathe. She used to tell me it wasn't ladylike and that I was breathing like a football player with big shoulder pads."

Lola's belly laughed followed. "That's a good one. Good ole' Peggy Pinkerton."

"See, when it's coming from my mom, it's hilarious," I pointed out just as I opened the door into the dog boutique.

"I'll be right with you." Vivian was just climbing on a stepstool to stack a pillow on the back shelf. The wall had every size, shape and color of doggie bed.

The shop was about half the size of my flower shop, but Vivian hadn't wasted one inch of floor space. One side of the store, the far more aromatic side, was stacked with bags of *gourmet* dog kibble. There were even separate bags specially formulated for certain breeds. A glass front refrigerator housed an assortment of fresh dog foods and treats. The other half of the shop was positively bursting with everything from dog car seats to specially designed steps that helped little dogs climb on the bed. The wardrobe racks were filled with every style, size and color, perfect for the fashion conscious pooch.

Lola grabbed a collegiate looking sweater that was big enough for either of us to wear. She held it up against herself. "Do you think this color would look good on Bloomer? He was cold last winter. I think his bones are getting old and creaky." She hung the sweater back on the hook. "He's been happy having my dad at home."

"That's sweet that he still loves him, even though Bloomer rarely sees your dad."

Vivian stepped off the stool and turned around. She recognized me instantly and smiled.

"Hello, Lacey, right? Or is it Pink? I was sort of confused because Elsie kept calling you Pink, even though you introduced yourself as Lacey."

"It's Lacey. Some of my close friends call me Pink. It's part of my last name. My shop is called Pink's Flowers."

"Oh, that makes sense. I was going to ask you about it on Saturday, but I never got around to it. What can I do for you?" Her expression changed. "I nearly forgot you were the person who went in to help with Ellen. I can't believe she's dead. Did they ever find out what happened? I left before all the action."

"It seems Ellen met with foul play. I don't know if the Chesterton Police contacted you—"

Vivian put her hand to her mouth. "They haven't. Am I in trouble for leaving the park? My mother needed help. She is painting her den. I didn't want her to climb on a ladder, so I told her I'd come over and paint the harder to reach spots."

"That's very nice of you to be so considerate of your mother." I smiled pointedly at Lola.

"Look who's talking, football shoulders," Lola muttered from the side of her mouth.

I walked to the counter where the sparkly collars were displayed. "You aren't in any kind of trouble. I just thought they might contact you because it seems the killer used one of your custom designed collars in the murder."

I'd probably blurted the grim detail out just a little too casually. Vivian's face paled and she looked close to tears. "I don't understand. I had nothing to do with Ellen's death."

I moved closer. "No, no of course you didn't. I was hoping you might remember who purchased this particular collar. It was a deep purple collar with pink rhinestones. Does that one sound familiar? Do you remember if someone bought it on the day of the show?"

Vivian regained her composure after hearing that her collar had been used in a murder. She lightly scratched her temple. "Deep purple with pink rhinestones," she repeated to herself. "That one is from my royal princess line." We walked over to the spinning rack that held all of her handcrafted collars.

Lola immediately grabbed up one that was leopard print with big silver studs. "Oh, I think Bloomer needs this," she said, holding the collar up to admire it.

"That's one of my bestsellers," Vivian said. "How much does your dog weigh?"

I shot Lola an admonishing look for yanking Vivian's attention away from my far more important topic.

Lola shrugged with a forced grin and hung the collar back up. "On second thought, my dog is more a cardigan sweater type than a leopard and stud kind of guy."

"Oh, I've got some really nice sweaters," Vivian started.

I cleared my throat. "Lola, why don't you go browse the

sweaters while we look at the collars." I gave her a look to assure her it wasn't a mere suggestion.

"Right, I'll go browse sweaters."

Vivian turned back to her rack of collars. She gently spun it around. "I'm thinking back to that morning. I did have one of those purple collars on my table, but I don't remember anyone buying it. I can make sure in my receipt book." She glanced my way. "I always write a description of the collar so I know which ones are most popular."

A slight charge of giddiness shot through me. It was entirely possible that I was going to learn the name of the murderer with this one quick stop at the dog boutique. The police hadn't even thought of this line of inquiry, so I was steps ahead of them. Before I finished silently patting myself on the back, Vivian emerged with a purple collar complete with pink rhinestones. "Here it is. I didn't sell it to anyone." She seemed relieved but then her mouth turned down in a frown. "Wait, I made two of those collars last week. This might have been hanging here in the store all along." She checked the entire rack. "I don't see the second one, and I've already hung the unsold collars back on this rack. I don't think I've had any collar purchases since then."

After that brief dip in my enthusiasm, I was more than a little anxious for her to check her receipts. "Do you think you could check your receipts from the show?"

"Sure, they're over here by the register." She brushed past the sweater rack. "What did you say your dog weighed?" she asked Lola.

"I'm not sure." My friend, who was always entertaining, formed her arms in a circle. "He's about this wide when I hug him, and he's about four feet long from nose to tail. That is an estimate. His current pillow is four feet long. When he stretches out his nose hangs off the end."

Like a skilled saleswoman, Vivian reached in and pulled out a large, light green sweater. "This one is warm and snuggly and can bring out the brightness in a pair of brown eyes." She handed Lola the sweater to consider and then continued on to her register. She leaned under the counter and pulled out the metal cash box I'd seen her using at the park. She pulled out an impressive stack of receipts and smiled. "I did pretty well on Saturday. Not as well as Elsie and her dog treats, of course. In fact, I can probably credit her with some of my sales. I'm going to ask to be her neighbor at next year's show." She paused and looked up from flipping through her receipts. "That is, if they don't cancel the whole thing altogether after this year's catastrophe."

"I'm sure they won't. Although, it certainly did end with a catastrophe." I stretched up, trying to get a peek at her receipts, but she was shuffling through them too fast.

"I sold the emerald green collar from the royal princess line but I don't see the purple one." Her mouth dropped open as she peered up at me. "I wonder what could have happened to it?" She shook her head and sorted back through the receipts. "No purple collar. I'll be honest, I don't remember selling it to anyone." She looked up again. "Someone must have stolen it. I don't know where else it could be." She sucked in a short breath. "The killer must have been at my table, and they stole it when I wasn't looking."

Lola had decided on the sweater. She brought it up to the register and held it up to admire. "Bloomer will look very dashing in this sweater. It'll keep those old, creaky bones warm."

"Great choice," Vivian said as if she hadn't plucked the sweater out personally. "I'm sorry I couldn't help you with the dog collar. I'm just stunned to think someone at the dog show stole from my table."

"I can think of something even more stunning than that," Lola quipped, referring to the murder, but I tapped my shoe against hers to quiet her.

Lola finished her purchase.

Vivian handed her the sweater. "I hope your dog likes it." She turned to me. "I'm sorry I wasn't more help."

"Actually, you've been a great help. Thank you so much."

"Can't wait to go back to the shop and try this on Bloomer. I think he's going to love it. *And* I think my mom is going to hate it. So it's a win-win."

CHAPTER 19

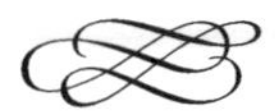

Ryder and Lola were still not talking by late afternoon. Lola had taken her doggie sweater across the street, without even stopping in to show Ryder, or, at the very least, say hello or I'm sorry. Which frankly, she pretty much owed him. I decided not to step any deeper into it. Lola's parents were leaving for Germany in a few days. I figured the rough patch would smooth out once Cynthia and John were out of the picture. I did, however, tell Lola that I would never forgive her if she didn't immediately send me a picture of Bloomer in his handsome sweater. And it was worth the threat because he looked not only adorable but the old guy seemed to be grinning with pride about his new outfit. I came close to showing Ryder the adorable picture, sure it would improve his mood but decided to wait. With any luck, Lola would send him the picture too. That might help break the ice.

The door opened and a woman walked inside. The breeze from outside caused Kingston to flutter his wings. The woman startled when she looked over and saw a crow standing on the windowsill. She backed up. "Oh my, I think I just let a bird in your shop."

"No, it's fine. He actually belongs in the shop," I said merrily. "How can I help you?"

The woman who looked to be about my mom's age hadn't pulled her startled gaze from the big black bird in the window.

"I assure you, unless your skin is covered in peanut butter or you're carrying hard-boiled eggs in your pocket, you're perfectly safe. Kingston is very tame."

She finally dragged her frightened gaze away from the crow and forced a weak smile. "Kingston? I remember my dad used to listen to a band called the Kingston Trio." Her hop back into a nostalgic memory seemed to shake loose any of the initial fear.

"Yes, I named him Kingston because he is very fond of their music."

She laughed. "That's a great story. I'll have to tell my husband about your bird."

I smiled at her expectantly, waiting for her to let me know what she needed.

She tapped the side of her head. "I guess your bird nearly made me forget why I came in here. I need a flower arrangement for my mother-in-law. She is in the hospital."

"I'm sorry to hear that. Hopefully nothing too serious."

The woman shook her head. "Just a gall bladder operation. Yellow and orange roses are her favorite."

"I've got some beautiful orange and yellow roses." I pulled out my notebook on rose arrangements. "Why don't you glance through these pictures and see which one you like best, while I go get the roses."

Ryder was heading out from the storeroom with a box of Styrofoam cubes. "I'm going to stack these under the potter's table so they're easier to reach," he said as he walked past.

"Good idea."

I went to the refrigerator and stepped into the chilly atmosphere to collect my vases of roses. We kept the colors separate. Ryder, the science guy, always insisted on keeping them in the color order of the rainbow. Of course, we had to supplement the green with poms since there were no green roses. I grabbed the containers of yellow and orange roses and stepped out of the refrigerator. Suddenly, there were more voices at the front of the shop, or at least one more than when I left. I couldn't quite make out what was being said, but I was sure I heard Hilda's voice. Hilda was a retired police woman who ran the front office and dispatch at the Port Danby Police Station. She was one of the nicest people in town.

I smiled and hurried toward the front to see what'd brought her to the flower shop. My steps faltered as I caught the distressed expression on her normally smiling face. She was struggling to catch her breath as if she had sprinted the three blocks from the station.

Both Ryder and Hilda looked at me with such grave concern, I had to place the roses down quickly or risk dropping them. Instantly, my heart steamed ahead of its normal pace. My gut instincts started doing terrible somersaults.

"What is it, Hilda? Has something happened?" I heard my voice, but it almost sounded as if it was coming out of someone else.

Ryder moved closer to me for support, but he left the task of relaying the awful news to Hilda. Her breathing was just beginning to return to normal. My head spun with the worst possible scenarios while Hilda collected herself.

She walked over but didn't get close enough for a hug or comforting touch. It seemed she wanted to keep her distance to keep from falling apart. "I had the radio on, listening to different calls from around the city." She swallowed. "James was hurt. They are taking him to Mayfield Emergency Center."

The room swayed. Ryder put a bracing hand under my elbow. "What happened? Is it bad?" My stomach was starting to twist and turn on itself making me feel dizzy and nauseous.

"I'm not sure the extent of his injuries," Hilda said. "Chinmoor is out on patrol, but he told me he'd call if he heard any word."

I glanced in the direction of my customer. She looked rightfully perplexed and upset. "I hope your friend is all right."

"Yes, me too." I turned to Ryder. "I've got to go to Mayfield Hospital."

"Absolutely," Ryder said. "Don't worry about anything. I'll take care of Kingston too."

I touched his arm and quickly discovered how badly my hands were shaking. "Thank you. I'll call you as soon as I find out anything." I raced to the office for my purse and shuffled frantically around in my cluttered bag for my keys.

Hilda grabbed my hand as I swept past. "Drive carefully, Lacey. Let us know the second you hear anything."

Tears glazed my eyes. "Hilda, he just has to be all right." I held back a sob and rushed out the door.

CHAPTER 20

The drive to the hospital was as long as it was short. The road stretched on forever and every streetlight was ill-timed as my anxiety built. At the same time, I wasn't sure if the short trip had given me enough time to work up the courage to walk into the emergency room. By the time I entered the emergency parking lot, I had worked myself into a fragile mess.

An ambulance was still sitting in the docks, looking official and scary. There were a number of police cars parked in the red zone. More than I wanted to count. More indicated something dreadful had happened. Maybe they were here for something else, I reminded myself, but it didn't help calm my nerves.

My phone had beeped twice on the drive to the hospital. I glanced at it. Two missed calls, one from Lola and one from Elsie. No doubt, word was out that Briggs had been injured on duty. "Injured on duty," I repeated to myself. "It will only be an injury and the doctors will fix him up and he'll be all better soon." I told myself that as my legs carried me, seemingly on their own volition since I couldn't remember telling my feet to move forward.

The massive glass doors slid open. I urged myself through

them. The emergency room was crowded with people, mostly sick, as evidenced by the masks contagious patients were asked to wear in the waiting room. More serious illnesses and injuries were moved quickly into triage to assess their urgency. I walked past the sickly looking people. Most were passing their wait time on their phones and very few were engaged in conversations. My mom was right, pretty soon no one would be able to hold a proper chat.

I willed myself forward and walked straight up to the window where a rather stern looking nurse with a tight black bun was seated at a computer. "How can I help you?" she asked brusquely.

"I'm here to see Detective James Briggs. I understand they transported him here with his *injury*." I added the emphasis to let her know that it absolutely couldn't be anything but an injury and preferably one that only required a few bandages or a splint.

She peered up over her glasses at me. "Are you family?" She went back to plucking away on her keyboard.

"I—I—We're soul mates," I said confidently after my conscience refused to let me lie.

Her face popped up and the tiniest sliver of a grin appeared. "I'm not sure what our policy is on soul mates." She pulled out a notepad. "What did you say your name was?"

"Lacey Pinkerton."

"Just a minute." She hit a loud buzzer and disappeared through a giant industrial looking door.

I paced a small, frantic circle around the floor in front of the window as I waited for her to return. Did she know anything? I was certain police officers didn't get brought in by ambulance every day. It had to be a significant event in the emergency room. I tried to think back to a few seconds earlier when I told the woman I was here to see Detective Briggs. Was she stunned or worried or trying not to show that the doctors would have terrible news for me? I shook my head to erase the dark thoughts.

A buzzer sounded and the industrial sized door swung open. The woman had returned. "Miss Pinkerton, this way please."

I rushed through the open door. It shut slowly behind us. We walked along a tile floor that was bordered on each side by small examination rooms, some blocked by a privacy curtain and others where the patient was sitting or lying in bed, waiting for whatever treatment was necessary.

Two police officers, a man and woman that I recognized as Mayfield officers, were standing outside an examination room where the curtain was drawn shut.

"How is James? How is Detective Briggs?" I asked when I reached the officers.

"Lacey, is that you?" the deep, familiar voice drifted from behind the curtain. The sound of it pushed an uncontrolled sob from my lips. "Come in here."

I took a deep breath to prepare myself. The worst was over. He was alive and talking. I peered around the curtain. He held his right arm against him. It was wrapped in thick gauze and bandages. The young doctor was leaned close to Briggs' face finishing a stitch right next to his eyebrow.

Briggs chuckled but cut it short when it seemed to pain him. "Step all the way inside. It's all right. The doctor is just finishing my Frankenstein transformation. They told me my soul mate was here to see me. Growing up, my soul mate was Sabrina the Teenage Witch. I have to say I was relieved to see it was my new soulmate."

The relief at seeing him sitting, breathing, talking and even joking pushed out a rolling wave of tears and shoulder jerking sobs.

Briggs' face was paler than usual, but his slightly crooked smile was still right where I loved to see it, on his incredibly handsome face. He put out his left arm and I walked to him. His arm circled me and he held me close. He rubbed his chin on my head. "Sorry if I scared you, baby," he said quietly.

"We're taking off, sir," one of the officers waiting outside the exam room said. "They're all in custody and booked."

"Thanks for your help with this. Good job." Briggs smiled. "I'd wave but I'm sort of without arms at the moment." He squeezed me closer. I wasn't going to complain.

They laughed as they walked back down the corridor. The doctor fashioned a bandage over the stitches near Briggs' eye. "I'll get your antibiotic prescription, and I'll add one in for pain. I think your arm is going to start hurting once the local anesthesia wears off."

I finally gathered myself enough to separate from his warm embrace. I stared down at the bandage wrapped arm. "What happened? Were you shot?"

His chuckle was a great sound to hear after the last half hour of panic. "No, I wouldn't be sitting here waiting for my release papers if I'd been shot. We'd swarmed the group and made arrests, but a thin and very sharp knife was overlooked in the body searches. The guy had it tucked in his shirt collar. When I asked him to take his arms off his neck so I could cuff him, he pulled the blade out and sliced my arm. He flailed as I moved to restrain him, and the tip of the blade caught my face." He pointed up to the bandage. "A half inch over and it would have gotten my eye, so I guess, all in all, I was lucky tonight. That is as long as you don't find me too disgusting to look at. The doctor said it's going to leave a scar near my eye."

I smiled and found myself leaning against him again. "Apparently, you have not read many romance novels."

"Not lately, no," he mused.

"Well, if you had, you would know that the battle weary, *scarred* hero always gets the girl."

"Yeah?" He pointed up to his eye. "So this is going to give me an edge with the ladies?"

"I'm certain of it." I kissed him. "Now, I'll drive you home and make you some dinner. Is there anything in your refrigerator to cook?"

"Hmm, that depends, is there a recipe that uses cold pizza and a half eaten pastrami sandwich?"

"I'm sure my mom could whip something up from those ingredients, some sort of stew or casserole, but as you know, I didn't inherit her culinary genius. I'll get you settled on your couch and then go to the store and pick some things up."

My phone buzzed in my pocket. "But first I have to call my Port Danby crew. They are all freaking out, waiting to hear how you are." I reached up and pushed his hair back on the side of his face. "I'm really glad you're all right, James." The earlier fright left a little waver in my voice.

"I am too." He took my hand and pulled me closer for another hug.

CHAPTER 21

I had to admit I was frazzled. It was amazing what a short span of full panic could do to a person. Of course, it was nothing compared to thirty stitches and pain medicine.

Once he'd been discharged, I got Briggs home and helped him change out of his bloody clothes into something clean and comfortable. I took Bear for a walk, fed him and tossed the ball around the small backyard for a few minutes before taking myself off to the store for some groceries. By the time I got back, Briggs was fast asleep on the couch. I fixed him a few sandwiches and wrote him a note with lots of hearts and Xs and Os (a momentary lapse into my teen years) and headed home to take care of my own pets. The whole drama had upset my stomach enough that I skipped dinner. After a hot bath, I went straight to bed with a book and cup of hot peppermint tea.

Morning had come so quickly, it felt as if I'd hardly slept. After spending a few hours helping customers and answering questions from concerned friends who streamed in and out of the shop all morning, I decided I'd earned a long lunch. It would give me a chance to check on Briggs, and since he conveniently lived in

Chesterton, it gave me an excuse to stop by Melody's Foxy Dog Salon. I was hoping to find out more details about the murder.

I headed to the salon first. That way I could eat lunch with Briggs. If he had pulled himself out of his painkiller stupor. Melody's mobile grooming trailer was parked out front of the actual salon. It was a tiny commercial space squeezed in between an office supply store and an antique shop.

A large, sad looking golden retriever was standing in a cage waiting for his turn in the bath. The dog looked at me with fresh hope as if he thought perhaps I had come to rescue him from his predicament. Melody was at the back of the room with her phone to her ear. She was facing the back wall and hadn't looked to see who had walked in yet. A cute, curly haired mutt was curled up on a pillow at the back of the room. The dog didn't even look up from his nap. "Just call me back, Barrett. I need to talk to you," she said before hanging up.

The name instantly caught my attention. She was leaving a message for someone named Barrett. It was a name I didn't hear often, yet I'd heard it twice in the span of three days. In fact, the only reason I remembered the name of Avery Hinkle's boyfriend was because it was so unusual. Could it be Melody had some connection with Avery's boyfriend? Or was she leaving a message for an altogether different Barrett?

Melody's gaze rightfully dropped to the floor near my feet. She was looking for a dog or some kind of critter to groom. "Can I help you?" she asked, slightly confused until clarity took over. Her eyes rounded. "You're the woman who helped me when I found Ellen—" She choked off her last words. "I never got a chance to thank you. I was so upset and such a bumbling mess. It was nice to have someone as calm and collected as you to help out."

Inwardly, I smiled about being called calm and collected, especially after my parade down hysteria lane the night before. "I was glad to help. I'm sure it was extremely distressing. I never asked—were you close with Ellen?"

She shrugged in a non-committal way. "I don't know if we were close, but I knew her well. There is sort of a tight knit community around the Chesterton dog world. You might have picked that up at the show."

"Yes, it did seem everyone knew each other. It wasn't all friendliness and warmth though, was it?" I decided to leap right into my questions. I was anxious to get over to Briggs' house to check on him.

Melody's lips curled in. It seemed I wasn't going to get much out of her. "I don't like to get too involved. There's a lot of backstabbing and—" she paused. "I don't know if you saw the scene up on stage."

"Yes, I happened to be watching when they picked the winner. I saw Avery Hinkle struggle with her dog on stage. Is it true someone gave Belvedere peanut butter? He did seem to be frantically licking his mouth."

"That's what appeared to happen. The judge couldn't really get a good look at Belvedere, so the trophy went to Pebbles. She's a great dog. She's always runner up to Belvedere, so the peanut butter incident was good luck for Ellen and Pebbles." She said it lightly, then frowned. "Oh wow, I can't believe I just said that. I mean Ellen's luck was short-lived."

"What are people in the dog show circle saying?" I asked. "Do they think Ellen was the person to feed Belvedere peanut butter?"

The golden retriever barked, reminding Melody that he was still in a cage. She walked over and plucked a leash off the wall, then she took the dog out of the cage. "Ellen seems like the logical choice. She was the person to gain the most out of a terrible performance by Belvedere." She walked the retriever to the area that was tiled off and set up with spray attachments for baths. The dog was reluctant to step into the tiled enclosure. Melody pulled a squeaky toy out of her work apron and tossed it into the bath area. The dog shot in to pick up the toy and while he squeaked away on his newfound prey, Melody calmly tied the leash to a hook on the wall.

I laughed. "That's a good trick for getting them inside the tub."

"When you've bathed as many dogs as me, you learn all kinds of tricks."

The front door opened behind me. Melody leaned to the side. "Carrie, could you give Riley a bath? He's all ready to go."

Carrie, a young woman with her hair braided down her back, walked past with two cups of coffee. She handed one to Melody and then went to the back of the room to put on her apron. Melody sipped her coffee and sighed with satisfaction. "I really needed this."

Carrie returned to the bathing area. She pulled a bottle of shampoo off a nearby table and opened it. She poured some into the palm of her hand. The warm cloud of steam rising from the bath wafted the citrus fragrance my direction.

I took a deep breath. "That smells good, like lemons."

"Yes, it helps mask doggie odor," Melody said after another sip. "I formulated it myself. Leaves their fur soft and fluffy."

"I thought everyone was using Ellen's Lavender Pooch shampoo. I have a sensitive nose I was nearly overwhelmed with the fragrance of lavender at the show."

"I don't use it," she said somewhat curtly. "It gives me a rash. I think this citrus shampoo is much better."

"So you're a shampoo maker too. There is certainly a lot of talent in the dog show circle. I guess that circle is smaller now," I noted, hoping she might have a little more to add.

"Yes, it's sad. I think it might get even smaller. I'm not sure what will happen if both of the top dog owners are out."

I stepped a little closer without passing her counter to hear her over the spray of water. "What do you mean both top dog owners?"

She leaned forward. "I know the police haven't made an arrest yet, but I think it seems pretty obvious who killed Ellen. We all saw the scene at the show. Avery was pretty angry."

I nodded. "She was, but do you think she was angry enough to commit murder? It's a pretty big leap from accusing someone of sabotage to actually killing the person." I was being devil's advocate, hoping to get more insider information about the group in general.

"Yes, it's wild to think Avery resorted to murder, but she does have a temper. I've witnessed it on more than one occasion. She has a short fuse. That trophy and the championship was a pretty big deal to her." She went back to her task. "But what do I know? I'm just a dog groomer. I'm not all that involved with the competitors. I just make their dogs look glamorous." She had changed her tone from accusatory to light and airy.

"I'm sure the police are looking into all possible suspects," I said. "I won't take up any more of your time. Thanks."

Her face popped up. "What made you drop by the salon?"

It wasn't a question I expected, but I quickly found my logical response. "Oh, I was in the area. You were so upset on Saturday, I decided to drop by and make sure you were all right."

"That was very nice of you. I'm still a little shaken but I'm fine." She lifted her coffee. "Right back at work, as you can see."

"Yes, indeed. Well, nice talking to you."

CHAPTER 22

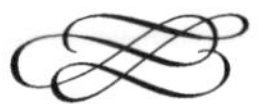

I had seen James Briggs rugged, windswept, and rumpled but I had never seen him disheveled. His hair was combed but not with its usual part. His wrinkled t-shirt seemed to be on backwards. Either that, or it was a new style with a tag sewn on the front. And, yes, it was summer, but we were not planning a trip to the beach. Yet he had pulled on his drawstring bathing trunks.

"I have learned something today," he said as I stepped inside and took in his interesting attire. "I've learned that my left arm is completely and utterly worthless, a mere appendage that I can use to hold up the left sleeve of my shirt. Did you know buttoning, putting toothpaste on a toothbrush and buttering toast are all impossible with one hand?"

I pressed my knuckles against my lips to stifle a laugh. "I'm sure it can be done. After all, there are one armed individuals. It probably just takes practice. You certainly can't blame your left arm for putting your shirt on backwards."

"Yes, yes I can. I noticed it right away when the tag started rubbing my neck, but it was so tough putting it on in the first place, I decided to leave it this way. Might start a new trend."

I walked to him for a quick kiss. "I'm just glad to see you up and around. Besides, it's kind of cute seeing you all vulnerable."

"Great, so now I'm vulnerable. What happened to battle weary and scarred? I think I liked that character stage better."

I walked the bag of cold sodas to the kitchen. "Again, you really need to pick up a romance novel now and then." I turned back. "Every battle weary, scarred hero has a moment or two of being vulnerable. It usually stems from almost losing the love of his life to some rich baron and it is rarely caused by not being able to butter toast, but in your case, we can make an exception. I thought we could eat those sandwiches I made last night for lunch." I opened the fridge and found myself staring at the cold pizza, now a day older. No sandwiches.

"Sorry, I ate both of them this morning. I think those drugs made me really hungry."

"I guess that's a good sign that you're on the mend."

He took my hand and pulled me closer. "I'm definitely on the mend now that you're here." He rested his forehead against mine, it seemed more for necessity than for affection. He was definitely tilting side to side some and his speech was slower and less crisp than normal. "Since there is no food, I thought we could take up the lunch hour with a little hanky and maybe some panky. Preferably both, since I've generally found that hanky is much better when accompanied with panky."

I giggled at his drugged attempt at seduction. "I think those pills are working just a bit too well. Maybe you should sleep them off. Besides, I'm hungry. I *mean* for food," I added before he could turn my words into something more flirtatious.

I patted his chest and stepped out of his embrace. Bear immediately slipped in to stand between us. He peered up at me with big brown eyes, pleading for some attention. I scratched him behind the ears. (The dog, not the man.)

"Did you drive all the way over here on your lunch hour just to check on me?" Briggs asked as he reached for a water glass. He grabbed one and looked at it. "What do you know? I found something I can do with my left hand."

"See, so you're not so helpless after all. You can still get a glass of water and drink it in your backwards shirt. And, to answer your question, I did drive out here to check on you. But to be perfectly honest, I also went by the dog grooming salon to talk to Melody, the woman who found Ellen in her trailer."

Briggs filled his glass. "Who is Ellen?" He shook his head. "Wait, it's coming back to me now. She was the woman with the bag over her head."

"I guess that spares me from asking the next question about what you've learned about the case." I headed out to his sparsely furnished living room. His house was decorated, using a loose definition of the word, in what I liked to refer to as testosterone basic. He had everything he needed to be perfectly content, no frills, no fancy fabrics, no stylish curtains or pretty paint.

I sat on his easy chair. He plopped on the couch as if it had reached up and grabbed his shoulders to yank him down. He lifted his arm. "Ouch. It's strange but it seems every nerve in my entire body is somehow connected to this right arm. This morning, I kicked the leg of the sofa, and I swear to you I felt more pain in this arm than in the toe that took the hit."

I couldn't hold back my smile. Nothing about the way he was acting was the usual James Briggs.

"You're laughing at my plight. Some girlfriend you are." He tossed the pillow he'd been using at me.

I caught it and fluffed it up. The scent of his shampoo puffed off the pillow case. "I can come back by tonight and bring you some dinner."

"I'll be fine. You might have noticed the long list of phone numbers on the refrigerator. Contrary to rumors, those are not women's phone numbers. They are a list of all the best restaurants that deliver food." His head rested back, and his dark lashes fluttered down. He was too tired to keep his eyes open.

I stood up and put the pillow on the couch. "Who started the rumor about the women's phone numbers?" I asked as I gave him a little nudge to rest his head on the pillow.

"I don't know," he said sleepily. "Maybe it was me."

He snored lightly as I put his feet up on the couch. I leaned down and kissed his forehead. I got a closer look at the stitches near his eye. The knife missed it by mere millimeters. The close call sent a shiver through me. I kissed him again, then pulled a bone out of the cupboard for Bear before heading out the door.

CHAPTER 23

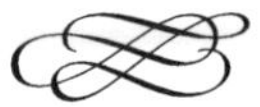

Sometimes my days were so hectic, the quiet solitude of my cute little house, or cottage as I preferred to think of it, was so wonderful I could almost convince myself never to leave. It seemed every acquaintance and their family had dropped by the flower shop, not to buy flowers but to find out about Detective Briggs. I knew in our small town, he was somewhat of a celebrity, mostly because he played such an important role in Port Danby's security, but the outpouring of genuine concern warmed my heart.

I'd called Briggs before I closed up shop to see if he needed dinner, but he had ordered Chinese food at three in the afternoon, so he wasn't hungry and was planning to go to bed early. I had been slightly relieved not to have to drive to Chesterton.

I picked up my plate with the gnawed crusts of a peanut butter and banana sandwich, a perfect dinner for a quiet night at home, and carried it to the sink. On my way home from work, I'd decided to contact the infamous Mr. Google (or was it Ms. Google?) to check for possible leads in Ellen's murder case. Since Briggs was not involved with the case, I was on my own. I needed to turn over leaves anywhere I could find them, and I'd discovered, many times, that there were plenty of leaves on the internet. It was a veritable forest of unturned leaves.

I grabbed my laptop from my room and sat on the couch. Kingston was fast asleep. Evening was always Nevermore's special mom time without the pesky black bird to get his beak in the way. Before turning my undivided attention to the computer screen, something that occasionally frustrated my cat enough to cause him to climb onto the keyboard and flop down, I spent a good ten minutes scratching his ears, the spot over his tail (his particular favorite) and under his chin, a place that always started up his purr engine. One thing about cats, or at least *my* cat, as much as he loved the attention, it quickly irritated him. After a prolonged rub behind his ears, he finally let me know the affection party was over with a swat of his paw. He curled up next to me and began his nightly grooming session. That was his way of telling me I could now divert my attention to my mundane human activity.

I opened the laptop and went straight to Ellen Joyner's dog grooming supply site. It was a nicely set up site complete with blogs posts from Ellen that discussed everything from giving your dog vitamins to etiquette at the dog show. Seemed as if her killer had missed that particular piece, I thought wryly.

Ellen's last post on the Friday before the show let her readers know that she was packed up and heading to Chesterton Park. 'Wish me luck' she said at the end of her post. Several of the comments beneath her post said things like 'Pebbles deserves that trophy' and 'this is your year, Ellen'. One comment went so far as to suggest 'maybe Belvedere will come down with a tummy ache or get gum stuck in his fur'. It always amazed me how rotten people could be in the comment section. They were always more brazen online than face to face, which was probably a good thing. I'd hate to see people walking around in everyday life completely at ease being as nasty and insulting as they were online.

Ellen's Lavender Pooch Shampoo had its own banner and top

spot on the page. It had over three thousand ratings and was at a very respectable four and a half stars. One bottle cost twelve dollars, which seemed pricey for dog shampoo, but the label boasted that it was chocked full of botanicals and oils "guaranteed to leave your pooch smelling like a field of lavender". That was not an exaggeration. It had taken me a good run of sneezes just to clear away the after affects of Ellen's Lavender Pooch, and that was long after I'd left the dog show.

I clicked on the reviews and scrolled through the plethora of five star generic 'great product, love this shampoo, my dog feels so soft and my little Bingley smells just like a field of lavender'. Bad reviews were few and far between, but there was only one single star review. It was from an anonymous review account that read —'I wish I could leave zero stars. This product is terrible. It gave me a painful rash. I would never trust it on my dog. Do NOT buy this shampoo!' the reviewer stated emphatically. It certainly did stand out in the stream of almost all glowing reviews. Interestingly, it wasn't the first time I'd heard someone mention it gave them a rash. It was exactly the reason Melody wasn't using the highly adored shampoo in her salon. Or maybe Melody had written the review. It might have been why she posted it anonymously, so as not to upset her friend. At least I thought they were friends but then it seemed the social connections in the dog show world were complex at best.

I moved on to a random search just putting in the name Ellen Joyner and found her listed on a lawsuit. Apparently, four years earlier, Ellen Joyner had sued, of all people, Horace and Belinda Crampton. I scanned through the mostly hard to decipher legal pages but was able to gather what the lawsuit was about. Ellen, the plaintiff, sued professional dog breeders Horace and Belinda Crampton, because as the suit claimed, she paid three thousand dollars for one of their standard poodle puppies, and the poor thing died just a few days after Ellen took it home. She sued to get back the three thousand dollars and legal fees. Ellen won the case.

I sat back and thought about the brief dramatic scene Lola and I witnessed as we ate our taco salads. A lawsuit would certainly explain why the Cramptons seemed more than just a bit put out that Melody had left their precious dogs in the pen while tending to Ellen's poodle. Since they lost the case and had to pay damages, the sting of that loss would not easily be erased, even though four years had passed.

I typed Horace and Belinda Crampton into the search bar and came up with a few blog posts from people prominent in the dog world. One of the posts took me to an old page on Ellen's blog where she was airing her grievances about the poodle puppy to her readers. The sudden death of the puppy had left her quite distraught. According to the post, she had been on a waiting list for one of the Crampton's puppies for three years.

I clicked on more recent blog posts, including one from someone who called herself Dog Queen. She wrote an extensive piece about the rise and fall of Horace and Belinda Crampton. They had been the breeder of choice for show quality poodles until the tragic fiasco with Ellen.

"Well, this is interesting," I said to myself. Nevermore was used to me talking to myself and didn't even raise his head. It sounded as if the Cramptons had had not only their livelihood but their entire reputation ruined by Ellen's lawsuit.

I found another blog post mentioning the once renowned poodle breeders had switched to raising French bulldogs. One of their puppies had gone on to win many top prizes. That would explain why they seemed perfectly at ease and accepted at the Chesterton Dog Show. They had rebuilt their business and reputation with an entirely new breed. They had also begun dog training classes that were, according to the many reviews, a great success.

I sat back to think about the information. It was easy to see why the Cramptons were speaking badly of Ellen Joyner at the dog show. They had obviously suffered great losses from the lawsuit. It apparently took several years to work their way back to the top. But they had done it, according to what I read. Could they still hold a big enough grudge against Ellen to kill her? Some people kept the thought of sweet revenge deep in their souls for years. Was it possible the Cramptons, even with their newfound success, still wanted that revenge?

I closed the laptop and patted my computer. "Good ole' Mr. or Ms. Google. You've done it again."

CHAPTER 24

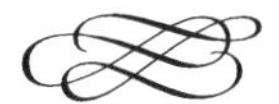

"That couple just put in an order for thirty centerpieces for a silver wedding anniversary," Ryder said as he popped his head into the office. "And they were both instant fans of Kingston, so I think your bird helped seal the deal. By the way, the woman, Charmaine, might have fed King just few more treats than usual."

I finished my last purchase order and got up from the chair. "How many is more than usual?"

Ryder looked sheepish. "I lost count after six."

"Oh my gosh, he's going to be a grumpy bird for the rest of the day." We headed to the front of the shop. Kingston had, with some effort, gotten himself back up on his perch where he seemed determined to spend the rest of his day quietly digesting his treats. "That's what you get, Mr. Piggie. Still, you get bonus points for helping us sell thirty centerpieces." I turned to Ryder. "White roses?"

"Yes, with baby's breath but we're only providing the flowers. They've ordered some specially engraved silver vases."

"That'll be elegant. When is the anniversary? Please don't tell me next week because I just finished the purchase orders, and I didn't order more than two dozen white roses."

Ryder picked up the order form. "The party is in October, so there's plenty of time. I'll go put this in the order folder. Then, if it's all right, I'm going to go to lunch early. Lola's parents are leaving tonight, so they wanted to go to Franki's for lunch."

"I didn't realize they were leaving already. I haven't had a chance to talk to Lola. Have things calmed down?" I asked as I straightened our card rack.

"Yes but only because they are leaving earlier than planned. Some rental house near the Alps had an opening, but they have to get there by tomorrow or lose the place." He walked to the back to put the order away.

I glanced over my shoulder as the bell rang. I spun around. "James, what are you doing here?" He had traded swim trunks for a pair of running shorts. At least his t-shirt was on correctly. "I thought you'd be at home—"

"Doing what? I couldn't take another second of sitting in my house." He walked over to say hello to Kingston. The bird hardly even moved his head in response. "What's up with you, grumpy?" he asked.

"He bird schmoozed his way to six plus treats, and he's now living with the regret." I noticed his arm had new gauze around it. "Did you go to the doctor? What did he say?"

"It's fine, just sore. I was feeling better, so I decided to head into my office to do some paperwork."

"Then, since you're up and a little more clear-headed than the last few days, we can discuss the dog show murder case," I said with just a touch too much enthusiasm.

"Whoa there, Sparky, what makes you think I know anything? I've been holed up in my house for a few days. The department makes a point of not bothering an injured officer with official stuff while he's recuperating."

My shoulders sank. "So you don't know anything? Not even a teensy smidgen of something interesting?"

"Sorry, I haven't talked to anyone. Like you said, this is my first clear-headed day since I got hurt." He walked over and took my hand. "But if I know my adorable investigative partner, she's probably got all kinds of theories and details."

I pursed my lips side to side. "Not sure if I should divulge any of my information since it seems that on this particular case, I'm working completely independent from the police."

"Lacey," he said with a raised brow.

I shrugged. "I suppose I can tell you since it's nothing too significant. First of all, I went to see the woman who makes the pretty custom dog collars, like the one found around the victim's neck. I met her at the show because her vendor table was right next to Elsie's. Her name is Vivian. That particular collar was from her royal princess line, by the way. In case that's of interest to you."

"Not particularly. Does the collar designer remember who she sold the collar to?"

"No, in fact, after she thumbed through her fairly detailed receipts from the dog show, she discovered that she never sold it to anyone. The killer stole it off the table. There were a lot of people that day, so it would have been easy enough to do."

"Guess that will make things harder. Although it would have been a fairly big misstep for a killer to purchase a unique, custom collar for the murder. And if you're already planning to commit the biggest crime of murder, it's probably easy to talk yourself into stealing."

"All good points. I know the main focus is on Avery Hinkle, the competitor who lost her trophy to Ellen due to sabotage. Her dog was fed peanut butter just before they went on stage for judging."

Briggs chuckled. "You have to admit, it's a pretty clever way to sabotage a dog show."

"Clever, indeed, but it might just have resulted in the clever person's death."

"So you think Ellen Joyner was the person to give the dog peanut butter?" he asked.

"I did find peanut butter on her shirt. The strange thing about that, though, is there wasn't any on her hands. Still, Ellen had the most to gain from the peanut butter trick. Avery was very angry. It was quite the scene. However, my sleuthing expertise, namely a simple search on Google, provided me with another person, or I should say *persons* of interest."

I'd piqued his *interest*. At least I thought I had until his worried brow crease appeared. "Lacey, don't start chasing down suspects. Especially with me being"—he raised his bandaged arm—"as you so aptly put, vulnerable and all. Leave this to the Chesterton Police."

"When have I ever chased down a suspect on my—" my voice trailed off. "Never mind, you're right. But this is different. I'm just going to talk to a nice, older couple, the Cramptons. They train dogs and breed champion French bulldogs."

"Did you say Cramptons?" he smiled at the name. "That's one that was sure to get a few good jokes in elementary school. How are these Cramptons involved with the murder?"

"The victim sued them for damages after she bought a sick puppy from them. She won the case, and their reputation took a hit." Just as I finished, the door swung open sharply.

Les didn't even say hello. He went straight for James. "It's true then. Linda Burton walked into the coffee shop a few minutes ago and swore she saw Detective Briggs head into the flower shop." Les leaned down to get a good look at the bandage around Briggs' arm. "I heard it was a sharp knife." Les looked up. "And they nearly got your eye too. But you got the guys right? Put them all behind bars, I hope."

"Sure did, Les. How are you doing?" Briggs asked.

Les waved his hand. "A lot better than you, apparently. If you don't consider all those big cholesterol blockages Elsie insists are squeezing the life out of me." Right then, as if she knew she was being spoken about, Elsie came nearly flying into the bakery.

Again, I was just an invisible entity in my own shop as Elsie walked purposefully toward Briggs. "Linda Burton just rushed into the bakery and said that Detective Briggs was in the flower shop loaded down with bandages."

"Linda Burton moves quickly when there's gossip to be shared," I quipped.

Elsie examined Briggs' arm and then tiptoed up to scrutinize the bandage next to his eye. "The skin isn't red or puckered so that's good. Are you taking your antibiotics?" she asked.

"Good lord, woman," Les said, "isn't it enough that you pester your own brother like a concerned hen? Leave James alone. He's not a child."

Briggs snuck me a wink. "I'm taking my antibiotics, and it's all healing fine. Thank you both for coming over to check on me, but I just stopped by to let Lacey know I was heading down to the station for some office work."

Les patted Briggs on his shoulder. "That's what you call dedication. Now that I've seen that our favorite detective is out and about, only a little worse for wear, I'm heading back to make coffee. Don't over exert yourself."

"Thanks, Les, I won't. I'll walk out with you." Briggs turned and winked at me again. "I'll talk to you later and stay out of trouble."

"Where's the fun in that?" I asked, then quickly assured him I was only teasing.

The men walked out. Elsie turned to me with a look of grave concern. "He looked pale. Don't you think he looked pale?"

"A little but then who wouldn't after being sliced and stitched all within a few hours. He's fine. How is everything at the bakery?"

"Great. I'm all caught up with my work after spending Saturday at the park. Did they find out who killed the lady in the trailer?"

"Not yet but Inspector Pinkerton is working on it."

CHAPTER 25

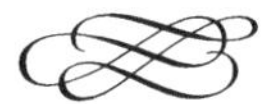

With my usual partner off the case, I relied on my other partner, the internet, to find out where and how I might meet up with the Cramptons. I was in luck. A quick search showed they operated their businesses, both the training facility and the breeding kennel, right out of their own home. It made sense that they lived on Maplewood Road just off of Culpepper. That area was all farms and old homes with big lots that were still zoned for agriculture.

It would be an easy trip to accomplish on my lunch hour. Their website claimed visitors were welcome which was all the invitation I needed. It would be easy enough to pretend to be interested in their training program.

I nibbled my homemade cream cheese and tomato sandwich as I drove along Culpepper Road. It was late enough in a hot summer that most of the pastures and vegetable gardens were already past their fresh green prime. Pumpkin patches were starting to become the crowning glory of the small farms I passed along the way. It wouldn't be long before the summer sun shifted to a different location over our pleasant planet, coaxing cooler temperatures and the explosion of fiery colors that came with it.

It was at that point in summer where I was more than ready to say good-bye to shorts and sandals and high temperatures. I looked ever forward to summer, but I was just as glad to see it trudge lazily away so fall could take over.

I turned on Maplewood Road, a small semi-paved path that rolled out between several farms. A sign at the end of the path was painted with the words H and B's Dog Training. While looking up the location of their training business, I'd discovered that they had called it H and B's rather than the Crampton's. That might have had to do with their struggle to rebuild their business after the lawsuit or it might just have been for marketing purposes. The name Crampton was sort of unique and memorable but it didn't exactly roll off the tongue.

I parked my car in the smooth section of dirt marked for visitors. The farmhouse was the typical turn of the century kind that lined Culpepper Road. It had an expansive front porch that curled around to the side of the house. The wraparound porch, charming shuttered windows and robin's egg blue front door made the house worthy of the cover of a country lifestyle magazine. I had to admit, I experienced more than a touch of envy as I walked toward the picturesque house. It was the kind of home most of us dreamt of, or at least those of us who preferred the quiet, bucolic life country living offered.

One of the French bulldogs, either Hamilton or Caprese or possibly even a matching sibling, was sitting on the top step of the porch staring down with his oversized eyes. His ears reminded me of a bat but the rest of him was all adorableness. Not that bats couldn't be adorable in some ways, to certain people, anyhow. I supposed it was the same with Kingston. I adored him and considered him adorable, but I had seen plenty of customers look askance at the big black bird as they walked into the shop. Then there was the *delightful* town mayor who despised my bird nearly as much as he despised me.

"Hello, are you here for a tour?" a voice called from an outbuilding. The voice belonged to a youngish woman who was wearing khaki shorts, a t-shirt and short work boots.

I walked her direction. Sometimes it was easier to get information out of an employee or friend than it was the actual person of interest. Her nametag said Sharon. In gold print, under her name, were the words 'head trainer'.

"Hello, yes, I just wanted to see the facility and find out more about the training program."

Sharon had glittery brown eyes and a nice wide smile. "Sure thing. I'm Sharon, head trainer. What kind of dog do you have?"

It was the next logical question and one I hadn't prepared for. My mind went straight to Bear, the only dog in my life at the moment. "He's a big mutt. We found him on the street. I'd say he's one and a half years old. We don't expect him to do pirouettes and make our coffee in the morning, just sit and stay and not steal food off the counter. The basics. Oh, and if you have any tips about dogs getting along with cats," I tossed in at the end, thinking I might as well make my lie worthwhile. Briggs and I still hadn't found the courage to put Bear and Nevermore in the same room after their first disastrous meeting where Never ran straight up a tree to keep away from Bear.

"The dog-cat relationship can be tricky, but I think you'll find once your dog learns the basic commands, it's much easier to keep him from terrorizing the cat. Although, I can't help you the other way around. Cats are their own masters, and, as you probably know, they don't take orders from anyone."

I laughed. "I have noticed that, yes."

"If you follow me, I can show you some pamphlets describing

the different training courses we offer." We stepped into a small office. A black and white French bulldog lifted his big head from a plush pillow.

"We're not here to see you, Sheba," Sharon said lightly. "Go back to your nap." As if the dog understood every word, she dropped her head and closed her big eyes. Sharon began to pull pamphlets out of a rack on the wall.

"How are the Cramptons doing after that terrible dog show on Saturday? I still can't believe how it ended," I said casually.

Sharon turned around with her brochures. "Were you there? It's awful to think someone was murdered right in the middle of all the activity." I followed her to a counter where she laid out the pamphlets.

"I was there helping a friend. It was my first time at a dog show. I assume they don't all end like that. Did you know Ellen Joyner?" I asked. "I saw her win the show. Then there was the scene that followed with Avery Hinkle."

"I wasn't at the show. I had classes to teach, but I heard the whole dreadful thing from Belinda. The Cramptons weren't friends with Ellen"—she gave a little smirk—"far from it, in fact. But they were both quite shaken when they got home. No one expects a dog show to end in murder but then there has never been such a blatant act of sabotage either. Ellen wanted to win so badly, it seemed she resorted to cheating."

"See, I don't know much about the dog show circuit or the people involved in it. I just thought the whole thing on stage, with the one woman yelling at the winner, was just a case of bad sportsmanship. So the woman who was murdered cheated her way to the trophy?"

"No one knows for sure, but it does seem most likely that Ellen did it."

Sheba woke from her nap and walked over for a greeting. I leaned down and gave her a good rubbing on her back. I was hoping to pick up the scent of her shampoo. I pretended to itch my nose after I straightened. "Hmm, I smell peppermint."

Sharon's eyes rounded. "Wow, you have a good nose. Sheba hasn't had a bath in at least two weeks, yet you can still smell her shampoo."

"Yes, it's very fresh smelling. When I was at the show, I noticed most of the dogs were using Ellen Joyner's Lavender Pooch. I guess the Cramptons don't like lavender?"

Sharon glanced outside the office window, but we were very much alone. It seemed I wasn't going to meet up with the Cramptons this afternoon. Sharon leaned a little closer. "As I said, they weren't friends with Ellen. They certainly would never shop on Ellen's site, no matter how popular that Lavender Pooch shampoo is. There was an incident a few years back, before I came to work for the Cramptons. Ellen sued them and the whole thing ruined Belinda and Horace's reputation. It took them a long time to build up trust in the dog show community again."

"Gosh, that's terrible." I pretended great shock for a second, then jumped ahead to my next comment. "They must have really hated Ellen. I guess there's no way to forgive someone when they've ruined your life." I was prodding, hoping to get some kind of a comment or reaction.

"I suppose," she said curtly, a big change from a few seconds earlier when she was free with her information. She shuffled the brochures around so I could see them.

"Be sure to mention our new Saturday afternoon group class," a voice said from behind. I now understood why Sharon had cut off her last comment so abruptly.

Belinda Crampton, the trim, energetic woman who reminded me a touch of Elsie, moved efficiently around the office, stopping to straighten the brochures on the wall before dropping a treat down for Sheba.

"Yes, I was just getting to that," Sharon said.

"It's my fault," I interjected. "We were just talking about Saturday's dog show. I happened to be there with a friend and well, I know I don't have to tell you that it was not what I expected at a dog show."

Belinda's mouth pursed. She shook her head slowly. "None of us expected it. Any of it, for that matter. People sometimes take the competition far too seriously. It's a shame when someone resorts to cheating."

"And murder," I added.

I'd ruffled a feather. Belinda was tongue-tied for a second. "Yes, of course, that goes without saying," she said abruptly. "That's what I meant, naturally." I wasn't completely convinced that she considered the murder the most scandalous, shocking part of the day.

"I suppose no one will ever know who gave Belvedere the peanut butter," I suggested lightly.

Belinda cleared her throat and busied herself with some paperwork behind the counter. She had a comment, but it was apparently lodged in the throat she'd just cleared.

I decided to keep the topic going. "Although, it seems Belvedere's owner was certain that Ellen had given him the peanut butter. She sure was angry at her."

"Yes, well one could hardly blame Avery. If Ellen hadn't given Belvedere peanut butter—" Belinda started and then stopped herself. "You know, I need to bring out a few more of those sign-up sheets, Sharon. I'll go print some new ones. It was nice talking to you." She forced a gracious smile and hurried out, seemingly worried she would blurt out more opinions about the dog show.

Sharon picked up a brochure. "I think you'll want to start this class first. It's for beginners. It will teach your dog all the basics. It's all explained inside the pamphlet."

"I'm sure you're right. Is it all right if I take this home to show my boyfriend? He'll want a say in Bear's education," I said.

"Absolutely. Our number is on the back of the pamphlet. Just give us a call and we can get you signed up."

"Perfect. Thank you so much for all your help." I patted Sheba on the back and returned to my car.

CHAPTER 26

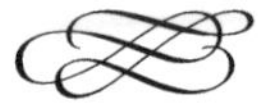

Ryder had kindly offered to drive Lola's parents to the airport so he left work early. I was relieved to see that he and Lola were back on speaking terms. She wasn't letting on but I knew my best friend and she was pleased that her parents were genuinely impressed with Ryder. As they should be.

I finished cleaning the work counters and walked outside to pull in my chalkboard and the cart of potted plants Ryder had rolled out to lure people into the shop. Voices drew my attention down the sidewalk. It seemed I had walked outside just in time to see Avery Hinkle and her boyfriend, Barrett, walking into Kate Yardley's Mod Frock clothing shop. Kate had a fun shop, filled with vintage items that were, for the most part, lovely relics left behind from the sixties and seventies. She also carried new pieces with the mod flare. I'd purchased a pair of go-go boots from her when I'd first arrived, both because I'd always wanted a shiny pair of Nancy Sinatra go-go boots but also because I thought it would help form a new friendship with the shop's owner. Unfortunately, even though Kate and I were somewhat friendly with the occasional polite 'how are you' we never formed any kind of bond. She was a stylish, no nonsense business woman who was slightly obsessed with men, most pointedly my neighbor Dash. They had dated at one time, but it didn't work out, at least not for Dash. Kate hadn't come to that conclusion yet. Even though they were both seeing other people, she still seemed certain that they would eventually end up together. For now, Kate was unwittingly providing me with an opportunity to snoop and eavesdrop on Avery and her boyfriend. Her shop was small enough that I could browse at any table and overhear what other customers were saying. So, *eavesdrop* was a strong term. I was merely overhearing their conversation because I would be in the vicinity. Of course, I was putting myself purposefully in that vicinity but that was just silly old semantics.

After a few seconds of wrestling with my conscience about listening in on someone's conversation, I reminded myself it was all in the line of duty. I was, after all, investigating a murder, even if it was not official. I had one big problem to grapple with. On the day of the murder, Briggs had introduced me as his assistant when he interviewed a slightly hostile Avery Hinkle. She had even rudely noted that she thought I was a baker's assistant. Her day had been eventful and, for the most part, terrible, but I had to assume she would recognize me. I raced inside and went to my office for the baseball cap I occasionally pulled on when my curls were out of control. I pulled my sunglasses out of my purse and put them on. They were a strange thing to wear inside but then mine did have a prescriptive lens. It was perfectly logical for me to wear them when perusing through jewelry.

Kate would probably be surprised to see me since I rarely stepped foot in her store, but I could easily pretend that I was interested in something. She had a lot of beautiful stuff.

I dragged the chalkboard inside but left the cart for later. Duty called and I didn't want to miss the slim window of opportunity to learn more about my main suspect, Avery Hinkle. It was certainly much harder doing this on my own without my usual partner. Briggs had access to all the suspects and witnesses. Without him, I needed to pretend to be interested in dog training classes and engage in other ploys to talk to important individuals. I had no such ploy in this case because I hadn't expected to see Avery. Hanging out while she was shopping was a simple way to find out more about her. I wasn't holding out much hope that my newest adventure would result in anything significant, but it was too good of an opportunity to pass up.

Avery and Barrett were already in the shop when I stepped inside. As expected, Kate looked up from her counter, where she was organizing necklaces on a rack, with wide eyes. "Pink, I haven't seen you in the shop in a long time." I was more than relieved that she called me by my nickname rather than Lacey. My real name might have tipped off Avery since Briggs introduced us. Avery glanced up from the clothes rack briefly and paused just long enough for me to start thinking of my response if she asked me about being Detective Briggs' assistant. But she went back to her clothes shopping. Barrett was leaning against a counter thumbing through things on his phone while Avery shopped. His disinterest was not going to bode well for my plan because it meant there would be little interaction between the two.

"Hi, Kate, I've been thinking about splurging on a new pair of earrings. I'm just browsing for now," I called back, hoping that would put an end to our conversation. I was wrong.

Kate strode over on a cute pair of pink short boots. Kate was the indisputable fashion icon of the town. I admired how she boldly changed her look every few months. At the moment, her straight hair was dyed a shiny black, and she was wearing long bangs. It was a little severe but it worked.

She stuck her hand out in front of me. "Did you hear? I've just gotten engaged to Brent."

"Wow, it's a beautiful ring." I would have been more surprised, only it was Kate's third engagement since my arrival in Port Danby two summers before. "Congratulations. Brent is the computer software salesman, right?" I asked tentatively. I was going just on gossip and a few casual interactions with Kate.

"No, that was Kenneth," she corrected with a sour expression. Apparently, I was supposed to keep up with the list. "Brent is a pharmacist in Mayfield."

"That's wonderful. It's always nice to have a pharmacist in the family. Again, congratulations. I'm sure you'll both be very happy." Avery and Barrett had started up a conversation, but I was unable to focus on what they were saying. I hoped my final wish for happiness would put a nice end to my chat with Kate.

"Thanks. Everything is still in the freshly engaged stage, but eventually, when I start planning the wedding, I'll drop by your shop to look through you bridal catalogs." Normally, the notion of creating flowers for an upcoming wedding thrilled me, but I was more interested in the conversation behind me, one where it seemed Avery was irritated with Barrett. In addition, since I'd known Kate to get engaged as frequently as I changed socks, I wasn't exactly counting on the business. Still, I hoped this one worked for Kate. She seemed to desperately want to be married, and it would be a relief for Dash.

"Absolutely," I said with fake enthusiasm. "Drop by any time and we'll plan the most floral-rific wedding this town has ever seen."

Kate smiled with satisfaction and pulled herself away from our conversation. Unfortunately, she carried herself over to her other customer, Avery. They immediately set about looking for the perfect dress for Avery's curvy figure. Barrett looked relieved to have Avery's attention taken away. He must have just gotten off work because he was wearing his orange shirt with the feed and grain logo. I was sure I saw a piece of hay stuck on the hem of his shirt.

My whole plan to eavesdrop on something interesting, something about the murder had been thin and full of holes. It seemed the only topic that would be discussed during Avery's trip to Mod Frock was which fabric suited her skin tone. She also made it clear to Kate that she didn't want anything that was dry clean only.

I absently fingered some of the earrings on the rack, wondering if I should just abort the mission. Barrett's phone rang, which earned a frown from Avery. He looked somewhat apologetic as he moved to answer it. She scowled after him as his long legs carried him out the door to the sidewalk. Kate was absorbed with the dress purchase. It was my best chance to slip out.

I headed out but slowed my pace considerably when I caught a rather impassioned plea from Barrett to whoever was on the other end of his phone call. "Please, you've got to stop calling me. Avery is getting mad. We're not going to meet. It's over." He hung up and pushed his phone into his pocket.

I couldn't delay my feet any longer without drawing attention to myself, and there wasn't any reason for me to dawdle now that the phone conversation was over. I'd left the shop thinking that it had been a total waste of time, but after hearing Melody leave a somewhat emotional message for someone named Barrett, I was convinced the name hadn't just been a coincidence. Maybe it was time for me to take a trip to Hart's Feed and Grain.

CHAPTER 27

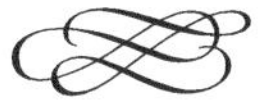

A summer thunderstorm had rolled in to the coast. It made a perfect setting for a quiet home dinner with Briggs. His kitchen was far too sparsely appointed to cook a real meal, so I bought some tacos and rice from a local restaurant. We sat at his tiny kitchen table, nibbling chips and salsa and listening to the rain and intermittent thunder.

He was looking even more clear-headed than in the morning. I could tell the shock of the whole thing had finally worn off. Now he just needed to heal, and that couldn't come soon enough. His usual five o'clock shadow of black stubble was quickly growing into a fully fledged moustache and beard. He said it was either a beard or more scars on his face, a probable result of shaving with his left hand. I wasn't sure how I felt about the excess facial hair. It definitely tickled when we kissed.

"I was thinking, after they take the bandage off and the stitches out, maybe I should incorporate the long ugly scar into a tattoo," he said. "Maybe a snake or something cool like that."

I was fairly certain he was kidding, but just in case, I decided to voice my opinion on his idea. "I'm going to give you a hard *no* on the snake idea. I get the whole manly, tough looking tattoo thing, but I've seen some really unsettling ink snakes and skulls staring at me from men's arms and shoulders. It's fine if I don't know the man, but cuddling with a snake staring up at me, that just doesn't sound fun. Besides, what have I told you about the battle weary, scarred hero? It'll be like you just stepped right out of one of my romance novels." I glanced around his small, masculine-ly furnished home. "There is one problem though."

"What's that?"

"That battle weary, scarred hero is normally holed up in his family's castle or estate. Is there anything you can do about that?"

He laughed as he dug another chip into the salsa. "Sure, I'll call my dad and see if there are any castles in the family portfolio."

"Great. Preferably one that sits along a rushing river and is surrounded by lush gardens. And no ghosts, please." I looked at him. "Maybe you should be writing this down."

He lifted his right arm. "Can't. I'll remember the list. It's not very often that I ask Dad for a castle."

Bear came bounding through the dog door, soaking wet and ready to spray everything and everyone with rainwater. Fortunately, we had planned for just such an event. Since I was the only person with two working arms, I shot into action. I dropped my taco, snatched the beach towel off the back of my chair and threw it over Bear like a shroud. He nearly knocked me over in his exuberance to be towel dried. The entire scene gave Briggs a good laugh.

"This is why I have a cat," I huffed as I rubbed Bear's head. His large body wriggled and twitched under the towel. I had to keep moving to stay with his wild, excited dance. "Nevermore doesn't go outside in the rain, ever. He just sits in the window and smirks at the pathetic wildlife that crosses our grass in search of dry shelter."

"I have to say, this is so fun to watch, I'm hoping Bear goes out for a second round." Briggs took a bite of his taco. "Look, taco eating, another task that can be done with my useless left arm."

The towel was damp and so were my jeans by the time I'd rubbed the excess water from Bear's thick coat. The odor emanating from his wet fur was potent. I covered my nose and squinted at the strong smell. "Samantha does not approve of wet dog. I think I might have to skip the rest of my taco dinner. I won't be able to smell anything but wet fur after this."

"Are you sure?" Briggs pretended concern as he reached for my plate. "I feel bad." He took a bite of my taco. "Really bad."

"Yes, I can see that." I carried the towel into his tiny laundry room and draped it over the washer to dry out. I walked back to the table. "Actually, the wet dog smell reminds me of something. I drove out to the Crampton's training facility. They're the people who lost the lawsuit to the murder victim."

"Yes, I know who they are. After you mentioned them, I called Officer Burke to see if he knew about the Cramptons. One of his assistants had just found it in his research. He was surprised I knew about it already. I told him it was my brilliant assistant who had uncovered it in a Google search."

I rested my arms on the edge of the table and smiled. "Did you really tell him I was brilliant? Actually, that's all right. Don't tell me. I'll just let myself go on thinking you did. I know I thought the Cramptons might be of interest, but I've sort of changed my mind. And it's all because of dog smells."

"Not sure if that's a great way to make a suspect list, but go on." He finished the last of the taco and sat back.

"The Cramptons don't use Ellen's popular Lavender Pooch shampoo. That makes sense, of course. You wouldn't shop from the store of someone who set your life back so abruptly. The dog I met at the facility smelled like peppermint. I didn't smell any peppermint on Ellen's clothes."

He rested his bandaged arm on the chair arm. I could tell it hurt more than he let on. I knew he'd decided to skip the pain pills because he didn't like the way they made him feel.

"Should I get you something?" I asked.

"A new arm, please. Anyhow, why would their dog's shampoo fragrance end up on Ellen's clothes?"

"It wouldn't necessarily." I got up and picked up our plates. "At least not in an amount that could be detected by a *normal* nose." I put the plates in the sink and went back to finish my theory. "But peppermint is one of those potent smells that Samantha can pick up even if there's just a trace amount of it. If the Cramptons had bathed their dogs with the peppermint shampoo, they would certainly have had some on their clothes."

"And if they had to tie the bag around Ellen's head, their clothes would probably have brushed Ellen's clothes," he finished for me.

"Exactly. Now there are enough variables, like they didn't use the shampoo on their dogs so there was no peppermint on their clothes. Or they were extra careful not to brush against Ellen as they pulled the bag over her head. Or Samantha missed the scent when I examined Ellen." I laughed and waved my hand. "We both know that last one is a long shot. Anyhow, I left the training facility with nothing more than some brochures for their classes. I could leave them for you to peruse," I suggested.

"No, thanks. Bear and I have our own discipline system worked out. He does whatever he wants, and I roll my eyes and tell him he's a goofball. It works just fine. Especially since he's finally grown out of the furniture eating phase." He motioned to the side of the couch with a scalloped edge that looked as if a giant caterpillar had gnawed it like a leaf. "Might even splurge and buy a new couch someday. Although, I *do* have the seat cushions perfectly sculpted to my bottom."

I laughed all the way back to the kitchen where I set about washing his sink full of dishes. "It looks like you were running an

Italian restaurant through your kitchen today. Just how many people dined here?"

"I'm bored and eating is my only form of entertainment." He managed to carry both glasses, stacked together, into the kitchen.

"Was Officer Burke going to talk to the Cramptons? I'd be curious about their interview," I hinted. "I was only able to talk to Mrs. Crampton for a few seconds. The one thing I learned was that Belinda Crampton believed it was Ellen who sabotaged the dog show by feeding peanut butter to Belvedere."

Briggs scratched his temple. "Not being on the case, I'm having a hard time keeping up with people names and dog names."

"Belvedere was the favorite to win, but someone slipped him peanut butter and that interfered with the judging. So the *favorite* lost and Ellen's poodle, Pebbles, the dog on the beach, won the trophy. Then accusations flew and Ellen wound up dead. That was my quick catch up summary."

He nodded. "Got it. I think I'll call Burke tomorrow to see how things are progressing. Even though I'm technically on medical leave, they'll probably need my help."

I put the plates in the dishwasher. An idea popped in my head. I spun around fast enough to spray water from my hands. He stared down at the splatter on his shirt.

"Sorry about that. I just got excited about a possible idea," I said.

"Excitement and new ideas from Lacey should always come with a warning tag. What's this new *possible* idea?"

I grabbed a dishtowel to dry my hands. "Glad you asked."

"Did I have a choice?"

"Not really." We headed out to his couch. "Do you think you could get me into the crime scene? I noticed the trailer was still at the park."

"Yes, I think they're going to move it to the evidence garage tomorrow."

I sat down. Bear climbed up onto the couch next to me and

dropped his big head in my lap. His fur was mostly dry, but he was still plenty stinky. "Then we need to go early before they move it. I'd like to search for more clues."

He sighed with resignation. "I know you'll just keep asking. I suppose I can get you inside for one last look around. Anything in particular you're looking for?"

I shrugged. "Nothing in particular but you know how second glances give you a whole new perspective." I sat forward, slightly jarring Bear from his nap. I patted his head and he went back to his snores. "That reminds me, I walked up to the Hawksworth site the other evening and took a second look in the locked trunk."

"At night? By yourself?" he asked. I loved that he was protective but occasionally it made me feel like a little kid.

"Seriously, James, I'm not a child. And you know how I feel about the dark. I walked up while there was still daylight." I pointed to my ear. "And yes, I just heard the irony there when I said I wasn't a child but mentioned my fear of the dark so you don't need to point it out."

"Fine, I won't. What did you dig out of ole Bertram's belongings? I thought you'd already shuffled through that stuff."

"I did but as I prefaced this conversation, it was all about taking a second look." Bear got too warm sitting on the couch. The cushions waddled side to side as he lifted his big body off the couch and dropped lazily to ground with a deep doggie sigh.

I brushed stray hairs off my jeans. "Remember I told you about the account ledgers? Well, I noticed an odd entry that was only listed as a gift. It was for seventy-three dollars. At first I didn't think much about it but then I found the same entry for a gift of seventy-three dollars for every month after. All the other entries were much more detailed with the name of the person being paid and their addresses and place of business but these recurring entries just said gift."

"Interesting. Maybe Hawksworth was being blackmailed or

maybe he was paying someone a monthly stipend but was keeping it from his wife."

I sat up with interest. "Which actually might link with the love letters I found. They are to Teddy from Button. Since it was Bertram's trunk, it's easy to assume he's Teddy, but Button is a mystery. Unless, of course, that was a pet name Bertram had for his wife, Jill."

"Could be but it sounds like you might be onto something with that recurring payment. You've become quite the super sleuth."

"So we're on for the trailer search tomorrow?" I asked with a hopeful grin.

"Sure. Who am I to stand in the way of an investigator and her crime scene?" Right then, a flash of lightning lit up his small house, light bulbs sputtered and the television cable box made a clicking sound. Seconds later, the power went out, bathing the house in complete darkness. I hopped over the cushion separating us and nearly landed in his lap.

Briggs put his arm around me and held me close at his side. "I planned that well." His voice drifted into the darkness.

I had no idea exactly when my fear of the dark became a permanent fixture of my psyche, but it had never faded. In my mind, something about the lack of light transferred to the lack of oxygen. But having Briggs' arm around me helped calm any sparks of panic that might otherwise have taken off like fireworks.

"Are you telling me you asked that streak of lightning to take out a power pole so you could take advantage of my weakness?" I asked.

"I might not have planned it directly, but when the thunderstorm started, I have to admit, the idea of a power outage did pass through my somewhat one track mind, several times. And it seems everything has worked out just as I hoped." He squeezed me closer, then winced as the movement caused him to brush his injured arm against the side of the couch. "Except for the big bandage around my arm and the twenty plus stitches. That was never part of my plan."

I rested my head against him. Raindrops drummed on the roof and the distant clap of thunder echoed over the town.

"I could almost get used to darkness as long as it always came with Detective James Briggs."

CHAPTER 28

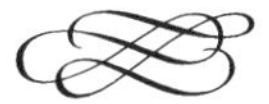

The police had put cones and yellow tape around the trailer, which still stood next to a grassy patch on one side of the park. The other side was busy with a baseball game and kids playing on the swings and slide. No one seemed too interested in the sad looking trailer and its belt of yellow caution tape. The shock of the murder had already worn off, and people were getting back to their summer activities.

The short-lived thunderstorm had left behind happy summer plants, once wilted and thirsty from the long, hot days. Trees and shrubs practically danced in the daylight, their thirst now quenched and the dry dust washed from their leaves.

Briggs had gone by the Chesterton station to pick up the key. The precinct was waiting for a special tow truck to pick up the trailer and move it from the park to the station's garage. While they didn't expect to find much more evidence, they had plans for a more thorough search once the trailer had been moved to their facility. So we were getting to it just in time. Once the trailer was at the station, I wouldn't have much opportunity to give it a once over. The quick stop at the station also provided a few interesting nuggets of information. Officer Burke told Briggs that the coroner placed Ellen's time of death somewhere between two and four in the afternoon. That matched with the time span in my head. The final trophy had been handed out around one in the afternoon, so obviously it had to happen after one. Melody had cried for help as the vendors were cleaning up for the day, which was around half past four. That left a pretty narrow chunk of time for someone to kill Ellen. In addition to the time of death being confirmed, when Briggs stopped in for the key, Officer Burke was waiting for the Cramptons to arrive for an interview. They had decided the lawsuit and subsequent personal and financial troubles gave the couple a pretty solid motive for revenge.

Briggs and I stepped over the fluttering band of yellow tape and walked up the portable steps. The short climb brought back the details of that day. "Do you know if Ellen's dogs are being taken care of?" I asked.

"Yes, Ellen's sister arrived and is making arrangements for the funeral. Burke said she is going to be taking the dogs back home with her."

"Poor things," I said. "I can't imagine what Never and King would think if I suddenly just disappeared from their lives. Although, if Lola took Kingston in, like she has promised in the event of my untimely death, then he probably wouldn't even notice me missing."

"He's still holding onto that Lola crush, eh?" Briggs unlocked the door and opened it.

"What can I say? Kingston is a romantic." The same smells hit me as on Saturday, lavender, a slight scent of blood and other dog grooming fragrances. Only this time, they were far more muted. No sneezes or watery eyes.

A light chalk outline showed where Ellen's body had been found. Not much had been disturbed, but the kitchen cabinets hung open and the trash can had been pulled from its space under the shelf. I glanced back at Briggs who was searching the door jamb for any missed clues.

"Did Burke say if they found anything of interest in the kitchen? They seem to have gone through it pretty thoroughly."

"He didn't mention any evidence other than the stake used to knock her unconscious and the bag and collar. The lab couldn't find any viable fingerprints in the trailer. They dusted the cupboards too and only found those that matched the victim."

I stood over the trash can. It looked as if it had been tossed around, not layered with the day's discards like normal kitchen trash. I pulled out the latex gloves Briggs had given me and gently moved the trash around. There was an empty yogurt cup, rancid smelling leftovers of fried chicken, the usual paper towel and napkin waste and an empty bag of turkey dog treats. There was no empty jar of peanut butter. One thing, completely out of place in a kitchen trash can was a number of business cards, just like the one Ellen handed us on the beach. There seemed to be about a hundred of them distributed throughout the rubbish. My guess would be that someone dropped them into the trash in a solid stack, but they were jumbled about when the police did their search. I pulled one out and checked the spelling and all the lettering. I couldn't find any glaring mistakes.

Briggs looked over my shoulder. "That looks just like the one she handed us on the beach," he said.

"Sure seems like it. I can't find any printing error or typo. I wonder why Ellen would throw away perfectly good business cards." I looked back at him. "Unless the killer hated that she had a successful business." I snapped my fingers, nearly ripping the latex glove. "The Cramptons certainly had reason to despise her success. Maybe they threw them out as a sort of symbol, a revenge ta da moment after they killed her."

"I've seen crazy little embellishments like that to a murder scene. You might be onto something."

"Great, I'd pat myself on the back, but I've been digging in garbage. Garbage, by the way, that does not contain any kind of peanut butter container." I moved forward to the open cupboards. "Now let's see if she has an open jar in her kitchen."

Only one cupboard had been set aside as a pantry. It contained canned goods, several types of crackers and a box of cereal. "No peanut butter," I said. "Not even a jar of its favorite companion, jelly."

"If she had sabotaged the show, it would make sense that she ditched the jar somewhere else, one of the park trash cans or bins," Briggs said.

"That's true. Only I still don't understand why I couldn't find any traces of peanut butter on Ellen's hands. Even if she had washed them, which she no doubt would have, I still would have picked up a faint scent. Peanut butter has a distinct aroma, and it's greasy enough to absorb into the skin."

"Well, if you're going to get all science-y, then I'd say Ellen wasn't the saboteur. Maybe someone else wanted Avery to lose the show. If she is always the winner, there could be a whole bunch of sour grapes out there. But then we aren't really looking for the peanut butter culprit, we're looking for a murderer. The dog show scandal might not be connected at all."

"You're right. It's almost as if you've done this sort of thing before," I quipped as I snooped around the kitchenette area for other clues.

Briggs' phone rang. He answered it. "Briggs here. Yeah, go ahead, Burke. What did you find out?"

I was all ears when I heard him address Officer Burke. I casually looked around but kept glancing and leaning my ear his direction, hoping to pick up the gist of the conversation. Briggs was not a man of many words on the phone, and this call was no different. "Right. That's pretty solid. Thanks for letting me know. Keep me posted." He hung up.

I clapped a few times in succession. "You said the word solid. Was it the Cramptons? Did they confess?"

Briggs chuckled. "Sorry to burst that bubble because it's awfully cute on you but no confession. A corroborated alibi though. It seems the Cramptons were not at the park between the hours of two and four. They had gone over to Mayfield to have a late lunch at their favorite restaurant, The Mariner. They frequent the restaurant enough that both the food server and the restaurant owner could confirm that they were there having the lobster, seafood platter."

My posture deflated. "Darn it. Thought maybe I had something there. But then, I did tell you about the whole peppermint dog shampoo thing. There wasn't any peppermint smell on the victim. I'm sure I would have detected it."

"Yes, you did preface your theory with that." He glanced around. "Have you seen enough, inspector? I should lock up and get the key back to the station."

"Yes, I'm finished. I need to get over to Port Danby for my other job." I sighed dramatically. "A woman's work is never done."

CHAPTER 29

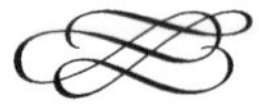

I turned my car along Culpepper Road and thought it was far too beautiful of a day to be driving a car. But my bike had not one but two flat tires, a result of an unfortunate encounter with a sticker bush. I still hadn't had time to get new inner tubes. It was probably for the best today since I had several stops planned and it was my turn to close the shop this afternoon.

It had been a slow morning at Pink's Flowers. Ryder and I had both puttered around doing small cleaning and organizing tasks we normally ignored. Free of her parents, Lola was back to her old self. Which if I really thought about it, was about a dozen different personalities. Most importantly, Ryder and Lola were back on good terms. That always made my life easier. Ryder had come back from a long lunch with Lola in such a bright mood, I had determined I could easily slip out for a few hours.

During the monotonous morning task of rewinding ribbons on spools, I had decided a trip to Hart's Feed and Grain might be worth my while. Barrett Hart's family owned the feed store in Chesterton. I had already devised a plan of getting him to open up about, of all things, dog shampoo. I was still going on the notion that Melody's friend Barrett, the one she had left a pleading message for, was the same Barrett who was seeing Avery.

Hart's Feed and Grain was in a remote section of Chesterton where the farms ended and the neighborhoods began. The storefront was a good sized stucco warehouse with only a few windows and a big roll up door. A large open barn was situated behind the store. It was stacked to the rafters with bales of hay and bags of feed.

A flatbed truck was being loaded down with bales of alfalfa. Neither of the two young men heaving the bales onto the truck were Barrett. That actually worked better for my plan. With any luck, Barrett would be working inside the shop, the appropriate place for a question about dog shampoo.

A woman in the orange Hart's shirt was helping a man pick the right dog food and another couple was picking out a bird feeder. There was no sign of Barrett. I browsed the line of shampoo and pretended to be confused. My act worked.

"Barrett, come on out," the woman called. "Someone needs help in the grooming aisle, and I'm with a customer."

Barrett was a nice looking guy with a slight overbite that sort of added to his charm. He had thick hair that he combed back as he headed toward me. He seemed to recognize me, but he gave me one of those 'you're familiar but I don't know why' looks. "How can I help you?" he asked.

"I'm looking for a good shampoo for my dog." I pulled a bottle of Ellen's Lavender Pooch off the shelf. "I've been doing a little research and review reading. I know that this is one of the most popular brands, but Melody, the owner of the Foxy Dog Salon, doesn't recommend it because it gives her a rash. Also the Cramptons, who, as I'm sure you know, are quite important in the Chesterton dog world, don't use Lavender Pooch. They have a special shampoo with a peppermint fragrance."

I stopped and gave him my best perplexed expression, hoping

he would add his own take on it all. He reached for a shampoo bottle that was tinted green and handed it to me. It seemed he was going to be the silent type of salesman. Darn it.

"This is the peppermint one the Cramptons use," he said succinctly, without wasting a word.

I unscrewed the cap. Without thinking, I pushed my nose over the opening and took a deep breath. It felt as if I had squirted a bottle of peppermint oil directly into my sinuses. It burned and made me tear up. I quickly handed him the bottle and cap before bursting into a sneeze fit.

He looked a little panicked. I put up a hand to show him I was all right. I shuffled blindly around in my purse for a tissue. I sneezed two more times and finished my embarrassing display. I was sure he'd never seen quite that reaction to a bottle of shampoo.

I sniffled and wiped my eyes. "Sorry, I guess I'm allergic to peppermint." I was going to use my explosive reaction to my advantage. "Obviously, that shampoo is out." I stared at the bottle of Lavender Pooch and bit my lip indecisively. "I sure would like to try the lavender shampoo, but I value the groomer's opinion. Melody was emphatic about not liking the brand." I looked questioningly at him.

He raked his fingers through his thick hair again and seemed to be debating whether or not to say anything.

"Have you heard any complaints about it?" I asked.

"No, most people like it. And, frankly, it's not surprising that Melody is telling her clients to avoid it. She is the one who came up with the formula."

I blinked at him for a second, not completely sure I was catching his meaning. "I'm confused (and I truly was). Melody came up with the Lavender Pooch formula?"

He nodded. I worried he was going to go tight lipped again but he continued. "Melody and Ellen were good friends. Melody was always mixing up new shampoos and grooming products for her business. She came up with the lavender shampoo and people loved it. I guess it makes dog fur really soft. I don't have any dogs."

"Then why did Ellen Joyner market it as her shampoo?"

"She basically stole the formula. At least that's what Melody claimed. Ellen was the one with the clout in the dog world. She started marketing it on her site, and people were buying it like crazy. We constantly have to restock the stuff on our shelf."

"That's not a great thing for a friend to do." I laughed lightly. "You sure know a lot about the whole Lavender Pooch scandal. I guess working here, you learn a lot about the dog world."

He nodded. "More than I care to know. I also used to date Melody. We were engaged for awhile, but it didn't work out." He turned back to the shelf. "Are you interested in the Lavender Pooch?" He pulled a bottle off the shelf.

"Actually, I think I'll give my nose a break from this aisle and look at your cat toys. Thanks so much for your help." And a grand slice of help it was, I thought wryly as I headed toward the cat toys.

CHAPTER 30

I was feeling slightly giddy that I'd uncovered yet another possible motive for Ellen's murder. However, I was keeping my investigative feet firmly on the ground. A possible motive with no evidence to back it up was just that—a possible motive. Naturally, my conversation with Barrett caused me to take a second trip to the Foxy Salon. I had no real reason to go into the salon, and it would be strange to use the same excuse that I was just checking on Melody to see how she was doing after the terrible day at the park.

My plan was still just a bunch of floating strands with no solid threads when I rolled slowly down the block where the Foxy Dog Salon was located. Melody's mobile grooming trailer, the one she had used at the show, was sitting in the side of the parking lot just outside the salon.

Before I passed the location, the trailer door swung open and Melody plodded down the steps with a bag of trash. She dropped it in the trash can sitting at the corner of the parking lot before heading into the salon.

A clear plan formed in my head. I dreaded the thought of going through trash, but it seemed Melody had just gotten around to cleaning out the trailer from the dog show. With any luck, the trash would contain clues.

I parked around the corner and out of view of the salon. I strolled nonchalantly along the sidewalk and took a detour to the trash can. The bin was at a sharp enough angle that it would be hard to see me digging through it from the shop window. The fabric store across the street was an entirely different story. I hoped none of the people inside noticed a perfectly respectable looking woman digging through trash.

I pulled off the lid and held my breath to allow the first and strongest odors to dissipate before I exposed my super nose to the smells. Fortunately, I wouldn't have to dig through much loose garbage. Melody was a neat and organized garbage thrower. Everything was in a trash bag, including the last one she tossed, which was conveniently on top.

I glanced around. I hadn't caught any unwanted attention, but as I pulled open the plastic drawstring, the salon door opened. Melody walked out with a sandwich, a bottle of water and the cute curly haired dog at her side. I pressed the lid back down. As she situated herself and her lunch on the bench in front of the shop, I stooped down behind the can. I was far enough away that she didn't hear my knee hit the can as I crouched into my hiding spot. My worry was—just how long could I hold the crouched position before my legs cramped up and the blood left my head?

I peeked up over the top of the can. Melody and her pup made pretty fast work of the sandwich. My feet were tingling with numbness and my knees were about finished when she crumpled up the sandwich wrapper. Adrenaline shot through me as I suddenly realized there was a good chance she would walk over and throw the wrapper in the can. I held out some hope that she would carry it inside to throw away because of her neat and organized garbage. Plus, the shop trash can was probably closer. She checked her phone, then pushed it back into her work apron pocket. She lowered her hand and allowed her dog to lick off any grease from the sandwich. The little dog was happy to oblige. I just hoped he would hurry with his clean up duty.

"Hold on there," I whispered to myself. The entire scene reminded me of the day of the murder. Melody was searching for Ellen. She had been walking Pebbles around the park as part of her dog walking business. The entire time Melody was at our table, Pebbles was busily licking her hand as if there was something tasty on her fingers. Just maybe there was.

After a good twelve minutes in a crouched position behind the stinky trash can, Melody walked back inside. Thankfully, she took her trash with her. I gave it an extra few minutes to make sure she wasn't coming back out before pushing to my feet. I pressed a bracing hand on the trash can as the blood returned to my head.

I resumed my trash search but decided to work quickly. I was pushing my luck at this point. I shuffled through discarded food packaging, paper towels, clumps of dog fur and a few empty bottles of shampoo and conditioner. I already knew that Melody used a citrus smelling shampoo in her salon, and now, thanks to Barrett, I knew the real reason why she avoided Ellen's Lavender Pooch. I was sure it had nothing to do with a rash.

I was about to give up on my quest when my brilliant nose caught the trace scent of peanut butter. I searched further and found a small plastic container, one that could be used to store leftovers in the refrigerator. I pried off the lid just to make sure. My persistence and my super sense of smell were rewarded. The container was mostly empty, but the bottom and sides were smeared with peanut butter. I decided to put the container back in the trash. There was nothing outrageous or strange about having a container of peanut butter in the trash can. It was a popular food item, although I couldn't remember the last time I made a point of moving a dollop of peanut butter to another container for storage.

As it was, it was nearly impossible to clean out a peanut butter jar for the recycling bin. That might have been why Melody tossed the otherwise reusable storage container. It would take too much effort to clean.

I gently closed the lid on the can and headed back to my car and to my hand wipes. It seemed I had possibly found the person who sabotaged Avery's win at the dog show.

It wasn't easy but I worked hard not to touch anything but my keys and a sliver of the door handle. I slid in behind the steering wheel and reached for the package of hand wipes in my glove box. I diligently cleaned my hands as I thought about everything I'd uncovered.

None of it was fitting in a logical, straight line. If Melody wasn't happy with Ellen because she made money off her lavender shampoo, why would she sabotage the show so that Pebbles would win? Or did she not care about who won as long as Avery, the woman who was dating her ex-fiancé, lost? Was her main goal to make sure Avery's dog didn't win the trophy? Or was there a more complicated motive to her plan. I still didn't have anything to connect the sabotage to Ellen's death. If Melody was the saboteur, and there was still no proof of that other than an unmarked container of peanut butter, then was she also the killer? What was her motive for killing Ellen? They were obviously on speaking terms. I had witnessed Ellen going into the Foxy Dog trailer for a grooming touch up. Ellen had even trusted her precious champion poodle with Melody. There were still too many holes. I needed to find a way to fill them in.

CHAPTER 31

Since I was in Chesterton and I seemed to be hot on the trail of something (I just wasn't sure what) I decided to head back to Vivian's dog boutique. She seemed to have her finger on the pulse of everything that was happening in the dog world. Just as I pulled up to the boutique, my phone rang. It was my favorite detective.

"Hello, how are you feeling?" I asked.

"I'm bored out of my mind, and I'm standing in a flower shop that is noticeably absent of one very cute florist. Her ridiculous bird is here, however, and when I walked into the shop, King noticed, apparently for the first time, that I had something white and slightly fuzzy on my arm. He swooped off his perch and landed, talons ready, on my shoulder to get a closer look at the furry creature on my arm."

"You missed a good one, boss." Ryder was laughing in the background.

"Yes, your assistant keeps asking the bird to do it again so he can get it on camera, but I refuse to recreate my entrance. Where are you at?"

"I'm in Chesterton," I said, deciding to forgo details.

"Of course you are, and I'm sure your visit to my hometown has nothing to do with a murder case."

"Nope, just cruising the streets, trying to imagine what the town would have been like with a teenage James Briggs running around it."

"Lacey, what are you up to?" he asked.

"A better question would be—what is Officer Burke up to? Has he found any good leads yet?"

"Not sure how that's a better question, but, to tell you the truth, I haven't talked to him today. I assume he's making progress. I know he was zeroing in on Avery Hinkle as the prime suspect, but he has little to go on other than the rage she showed Ellen in front of the entire dog show audience."

I rolled down the window to let some air in the hot car. "I'm beginning to think that Ellen did not sabotage the dog show."

"Is that so?" The familiar squeak that came through the phone was one of the stools in the shop. He had sat down at the work island. "Go away, you daft bird. It's only a bandage."

I laughed. "Maybe we should glue some googly eyes on that thing. It'll really freak him out."

"That might be fun for you, but it won't be too fun for the guy in the bandage. And you're avoiding the subject. Who do you think sabotaged the dog show?"

"I've found a few clues and motives here and there, but I don't want to take time out of my break to tell you. I've got one more stop to make, then I'm heading back to the shop. Will you still be there?"

"Probably not. I told Hilda I'd bring her some lunch. She hasn't had a chance to step away from her desk all day. Don't do anything dangerous. I'll expect a full debriefing tonight."

"Yes, sir, and keep that fuzzy arm of yours away from birds of prey," I chuckled as I hung up.

I got out of my car and walked into the shop. Vivian was helping a customer fit her tiny dog with a harness. She glanced up to see who had walked inside. I immediately sensed a chill in her demeanor as if she wasn't too thrilled to see me. I braced for an icy reception.

I browsed the dog treats, thinking it might help if I bought something from the store. I found a treat that had a variety of meats and vegetables in its all organic formula. I decided to buy two bags, one for Bear and one for Kingston.

Vivian rang up the dog harness. The customer walked happily out with her tiny pooch. "I didn't expect to see you here again," Vivian said with a dry tone. "I've already talked to the police. They came here the day before yesterday to find out about the dog collar." That explained some of her unfriendliness. She might even have decided that I told the police that the collar came from her boutique.

I put on a cheery smile and placed my two bags of treats on the counter. "I guess it's good that you'd already figured out it was stolen. I'm sure it would have been nerve wracking to look for it with police officers milling about the store."

"It was nerve wracking anyhow," she said curtly and started to ring up the treats. "I don't understand how I got pulled into this awful mess. I'm just a business woman trying to make a living. My customers just happened to be part of the dog show world."

I pulled out my wallet. "I'm sure it's the last thing you wanted. Have you seen any of them?" I asked as I handed her my debit card. "I mean, have you talked to Avery or anyone?"

She was put off by my question. She dragged my card quickly through the card reader. "I've talked to Avery. She is not at all happy to be dragged into this either. It's a big mess and all because Ellen decided to sabotage the dog show."

It seemed strange that she took the conversation back to the sabotage. I wondered if Avery was still obsessing about her loss. "I guess Avery is still convinced that Ellen ruined Belvedere's chances."

"I'm sure of it. Who else would have done it?" She handed me back the card. "But that doesn't mean Avery killed Ellen. She's already talked to the police. She told them she had nothing to do with it."

I nodded. "Quick question, since you know most of the dog people around here. Were Ellen Joyner and Melody Langley good friends? I remember Melody was walking Pebbles for Ellen at the show. Did they hang out much?"

She wore a suspicious expression as she handed me the bag with the dog treats. "Are you working with the police or something? As you said, I know a lot of the dog people in Chesterton. They're my customers. I don't want to do or say anything to lose their trust."

"I understand completely." I looked down with a disappointed frown. "I was just curious about their relationship," I said resignedly.

"Well, it wasn't good," she said with some exasperation as if I'd pestered her to no end. "Melody came up with the idea for Lavender Pooch, but Ellen marketed it as her own and made a small fortune. That would hardly lead to a good friendship."

"Yes, I suppose that would make them enemies." I watched her reaction to see if there was any spark, something that might show she was suddenly considering that Melody might have killed Ellen. She didn't even seem to consider it.

"Well, I've got to get back to work," she said sharply.

I lifted the bag of treats. "Yes, and I've got some treats to give out. Thank you." I walked out and headed to my car. As I climbed inside, a car pulled up to the boutique. I started my car and pulled away. I reached up to adjust my mirror and noticed that Melody was the person getting out of the car at the boutique. After my rather cold dismissal, it would probably cause a scene if I walked back into the shop. Since I didn't have my usual official partner, it wasn't as if I could just ask Melody questions about the day of the murder.

"Poo," I sighed. If I had gotten to the store ten minutes later, I would have casually run into Melody. Not that I would have known what to say or ask her to help dig out details.

I drove down the small street of shops and a new thought occurred to me. Occasionally, coworkers were a good, unwitting source of information. If Melody was at the boutique, it was likely that I'd find her assistant, Carrie, alone in the store. One more stop before I headed back to my own shop.

CHAPTER 32

I had to remind myself that I was just flailing about with this case. It was so much harder solving a murder without Briggs and without having any real right to investigate it. My unexpectedly cold reception from the otherwise friendly Vivian was a good slap in the face. People weren't interested in someone nosing around in their social circle, particularly after one prominent member had been killed and several other prominent members were likely suspects. I was treading on tender ground. No one wanted to be thought of as a tattle tale, especially when murder was involved.

I was certain Melody's assistant wouldn't remember me after my brief visit to the salon. She mostly saw me from the back (not my best side) and once she walked into the work area, she set right to work pulling on an apron to bathe a dog. I was going to head into the salon with a question about dog shampoos, a topic that seemed to have significance in the case. Chances were it would lead to absolutely nothing, but it was my only opportunity to talk to someone who knew Melody and who was far from the fray of Saturday's murder.

I parked around the corner again, in case I had to make a sneaky get away. I had no idea how long Melody would be out of the salon. As I walked around the corner and past the mobile salon trailer, a woman was just leaving, a good sign that I would catch the assistant without a customer.

The sharp repetitive sound of a small dog barking pierced the air as I walked inside. The humid, hot and fragrance laden atmosphere sprang me into a short sneeze fit.

"Do you need a tissue?" Carrie had to raise her voice to be heard over the dog's incessant yapping. She was holding out a tissue, which I accepted with a smile and nod.

"It's the grooming products," Carrie said loudly. "They make a lot of people sneeze."

"Yes, I have a sensitive nose," I said at a tone that was just short of yelling. It was like trying to hold a conversation at a rock concert. I motioned toward the tiny Pomeranian who was dancing around the cage barking toward every corner. "That's a lot of volume for such a small dog," I said loudly.

"The little ones are always the loudest, and they never stop for a breath." Carrie held up a finger, signaling just a minute. She reached under the counter and lifted out a large cookie jar. She opened the lid. The earthy smell of peanut butter cut through the perfume in the air. She pulled out a pillowy shaped dog treat and tossed it into the cage. The tiny ball of fluff immediately quieted down as it gobbled up the treat.

"Guess that'll help for a few seconds," I noted.

"More than a few. It's one of Melody's inventions. They are pill pockets that people use to give their dogs medicine. We fill them with peanut butter. It takes them awhile to lick the stuff off their teeth and gums."

I blinked at her a few seconds, stunned by what I'd just heard. On my first visit to the salon, Melody had used a toy to lure a big dog into the bath. She had boasted about working with dogs long enough that she knew a lot of tricks.

"Very interesting," I finally choked out. "I guess whatever works, eh?"

"Yes, now we probably only have about three minutes until Chloe is finished with her treat. What can I do for you? I have a price list if that's why you stopped in."

"Yes, that would be great." The peanut butter filled pocket had thrown me off my game. My mind was dashing about, trying to decide whether Melody's trick was evidence that she sabotaged the show or whether it gave her good reason to have a mostly empty container of peanut butter in her trash.

Carrie pulled a price list out of a drawer and handed it to me. I decided to use my last few minutes in the shop wisely.

"Thank you, this will help. How is Melody doing? I was reading in the paper about the murder at the dog show. It mentioned that she was the person to discover the body. Was she good friends with the lady who was killed?"

Carrie was young, maybe nineteen. It was possible she hadn't worked long at the salon. The grim topic didn't seem to change her demeanor. "I guess she's all right. Melody has hardly talked about it. We've been pretty busy. Ellen was an occasional customer, but I don't think they were friends or anything. Is that all you need?" Just as she asked it, the dog started up its shrill concert.

I lifted the paper and nodded. "Yes, thanks," I said loudly and walked out the door.

CHAPTER 33

The rest of the day was taken up by an excited bride-to-be looking for the perfect floral arrangements for her December wedding. After much consideration, she decided on large bouquets overflowing with red roses and white anemones held together by pale wintergreen eucalyptus leaves. It was the perfect choice for her winter wedding.

Ryder took off an hour before closing to help Lola rearrange her store back to the way it looked pre-parent visit. Apparently, she and her mom had vastly different opinions on the flow and layout of an antique shop.

By the time the bride left the flower shop, the sun was setting and Lola's Antiques was dark and closed for the night. Elsie and Les had closed up for the night too. The lingering aromas of freshly brewed coffee and fresh baked goods had floated up and away leaving me with just the floral perfume that was a permanent part of the shop atmosphere.

I walked into the office to finish up a few things on the computer. With my afternoon taken up by wedding bouquets, I hadn't had a chance to think about my trip to Chesterton. I certainly hadn't stumbled upon anything earth shattering, but my mind kept popping back to the *trick* Melody and her assistant used to quiet down barking dogs. It was rather coincidental that the person who sabotaged the dog show just happened to use peanut butter, knowing that Belvedere would spend a good deal of time obsessively licking his teeth and gums to finish off the sticky mess. Most people, even non-dog people, knew that it was rather comical to watch a dog eat peanut butter. I'd had more than one viral peanut butter dog video pushed my way. I'd even seen it on a peanut butter commercial. But if I were trying to ruin a dog's chance at first place in a dog show, I doubt my mind would go straight to peanut butter. A couple of cats or a recorded fire truck siren or even a dog whistle but peanut butter wouldn't even make the top three on my list.

The bell on the door clanged. I was regretting not turning over the closed sign and locking the door when I'd walked back to the office. I headed to the front and was more than surprised to find Avery Hinkle standing in the center of my store. From the harsh expression on her face, she wasn't there to buy flowers.

"Just who do you think you are?" she blurted before I could even say hello. "I know the detective introduced you as his assistant, but why on earth are you going around Chesterton asking people about me?" She walked straight toward me at an angry enough pace that Kingston woke from his nap. He danced nervously across his perch as he sensed the tension in the room.

"I wasn't asking about you so much as I was trying to find out details about the day of the murder." I spoke calmly, hoping some of it would rub off on her, but her nostrils flared wider and she moved closer. Her eyes flicked toward Kingston. She didn't look too thrilled about being stared at by a seemingly agitated crow. I wondered briefly if Kingston was the only thing keeping her from hauling off and hitting me. I'd seen her temper in full action at the show. I was getting a second view of it right in my own shop.

Avery pointed a long pink nail at me. Her finger came close enough that it nearly touched my nose. "Vivian said you've been asking about me. Then Barrett calls to let me know the lady who was with the cop at the dog show was snooping around the feed store pretending to look for dog shampoo."

"Actually, I was looking for a shampoo that didn't make me sneeze." She saw right through my thin lie.

"Really." She pointed at Kingston. He sat up at attention. "Because I don't think crows need dog shampoo. And who keeps a creepy crow in a flower shop?" She paused and looked his direction. "Is he dangerous?"

"He can be if he thinks someone is threatening me." I decided to keep up the guise that Kingston could somehow protect me. Anger was still coming off of her in waves.

She leaned forward and pulled her lips in tight. "He better not come near me. And *you* better stay far away from my friends. The police have already questioned everyone. No more sneaking around, trying to pin this murder on me. I've already told the police I didn't do it."

I shrugged. It had been a long day, and her rudeness and threats were starting to irritate me. "Well then, that's that. I guess since you've declared yourself innocent, the police should just look elsewhere. After all, that's usually how it works."

"I am innocent. First, Ellen robbed me of the trophy, then someone decided to kill her because she's a cheat. She has cheated a lot of people out of their businesses and money. I didn't kill Ellen, but I'm certainly not crying tears for her. I'm just wondering what your part is in all this? Why are you so interested in the case?"

"As Detective Briggs said, I'm his assistant. I have a *skill* that comes in handy when evidence is being collected. I help the police out on murder cases."

Avery was, in general, an attractive woman, but rage did not look good on her. Her whole face bunched up and turned into a puffy red tomato. "I think your only skill is being nosy. Stay away from my friends and stop asking questions about me."

She moved closer. I instinctively stepped back.

Knowing she had scared me, made her grin wickedly. "Unless you are officially part of the police force, I don't want to hear that you've been around any of my friends again."

"Have you ever heard the phrase 'methinks the lady doth protest too much'?"

Avery's angry face contorted to confusion. Obviously, the woman had never been asked to read *Hamlet* in high school.

The confusion was quickly washed away by more anger. "I don't know what you're getting at with your gibberish."

"I think Shakespeare might have a quibble with you calling his words gibberish, but I suppose I should tell you that I don't think you killed Ellen. And I don't think Ellen gave Belvedere peanut butter. The person who killed Ellen and the person who ruined your chances at a trophy are one in the same. At least, that is my theory, but since you want me to back off and stay away from the case, I'll just keep my well-founded suspicions locked up right under my nosy nose." I turned the invisible key.

Some of the color had drained from her ruddy complexion. "What do you mean? Of course Ellen gave peanut butter to Belvedere. She wanted the trophy. She knew the only person she had to beat was me. She's the one who benefited the most."

"I guess that's the simple truth then. Ellen gained the most from your dog losing the trophy, so she must have given him the peanut butter." I was probably toying too much with a woman who obviously had the temper of a storm at sea, but she had been far too rude to deserve any kind of civilized discussion.

"Of course she did it," Avery said, sounding a little unsure. I leaned back from a small spray of spittle that flew from her lips. "She was the only person with motive."

"So there was no one else at the dog show that day who might hold a grudge or dislike you for some reason?" (I, myself, could think of a lot of reasons to dislike Avery.)

Her mouth pursed and her face reddened. We were back to full anger. "I'm highly respected with the dog show set. No one would have purposefully caused Belvedere to lose except Ellen."

"Then who hated Ellen enough to kill her? The entire show audience saw you yelling at Ellen. I suppose you can see why the police were questioning you."

Avery's angry words got tangled on her tongue. "I told you, they've questioned me, and I didn't do it. Don't you dare think about accusing me again."

"That wasn't an accusation. As I told you before, I don't think you killed Ellen. Just like I don't think Ellen gave Belvedere peanut butter." I'd had enough of the conversation. She was too angry to even hear my words.

"This has been a lovely chat," I said with a good dollop of sarcasm. "I'm about to close up for the night."

For a brief, scary second, I thought she wasn't going to leave. What if my new theory was wrong and Avery had killed Ellen? The murder was particularly vicious and calculated. Avery's temper made her a bit more suspect. What if I was staring down a killer? I weighed my options for escaping a brutal attack. There weren't many except screaming and fighting back.

I released a breath when Avery turned sharply on her heels and marched to the door. "Just stay out of my life," she said with a fierce scowl before walking out.

I wasted no time locking up.

CHAPTER 34

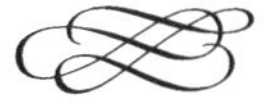

A low thud sounded on the bottom of the door. After my unsettling visit from Avery, I made sure to peek through the peephole. Briggs was holding a bottle of wine and a bucket of fried chicken with his left arm, leaving him with no hand to knock.

I pulled open the door and took the bucket of chicken from his hand.

"I had to kick the door because I was without a knocking hand," he said as he carried the bottle of wine to the table.

"Yes, I puzzled that out before I opened the door." I went to the kitchen to pull down a few plates and glasses.

"So, the higher ups have told me I can't go back on duty until all the stitches are out."

I spun around with the plates. "Of course you can't. Did you actually call and try to get off of sick leave? You, my friend, are married to your job." I put the plates on the table. "How on earth would you be able to do police work when knocking on a door is a chore?"

"I blame that on the bucket of chicken. I wasn't planning to go out on patrol. I was just hoping to comb through some cases and analyze evidence."

I grabbed a corkscrew from the kitchen drawer. I was known for my complete destruction of a cork before actually getting it open, so the job always fell to Briggs. We both stared at the tightly sealed wine bottle for a few seconds.

"I think I have a few of your beers in the fridge," I suggested.

"That's probably easier than watching you massacre a plug of cork."

I walked back to the refrigerator, pulled out a beer and returned to the table.

I sat down across from him. "I know this has been a big setback for you, James, but I have to say, having you off work and free to come over in the evening for dinner has been pretty cool. Normally, you're so busy, we're lucky if we can squeeze in a rushed lunch at Franki's. Guess that makes me seem selfish but I don't care. I like getting to see you more."

His smile over a bucket of fried chicken was extra wonderful. "I have to agree, it has been one of the perks of getting hurt. Now if I could just find something to keep me from going stir crazy when I'm sitting at home."

I plucked a drumstick out of the bucket. "Well, if you want to be part of my unofficial investigation into the dog show murder, I've got a few new details."

"Why am I not surprised? By the way, Officer Burke caught me up on the *official* investigation today. Although, based on your cute, smug grin, something tells me the unofficial one is already miles ahead of the official one. What have you found out?"

I shook my head. "Nope, since you brought up the official investigation, you first. I want to hear if we're on the same path."

"It seems they are focused on Avery Hinkle. She was seen screaming and yelling at the victim just hours before because she lost the dog show." He smirked. "Can you imagine risking life in prison because of a dog show trophy? Anyhow, turns out the bag used to suffocate Ellen had Avery's fingerprints all over it."

"Yes because it belonged to her," I interjected. "That doesn't seem too solid in the evidence department."

"Then there's the fact that she was seen near Ellen's trailer. And the girl who was walking the dog—I forget her name."

"Melody," I said.

Briggs grunted in frustration. "See, my mind is slipping because I'm not working. The same thing happened to my grandfather. He retired from his job as an air traffic controller and two months later, he could hardly remember my name."

I tilted my head. "James, don't be silly. A few weeks off from work is not going to send you straight into dementia. You've probably still got a few good years left before you start leaving your car keys in the freezer."

"Thanks, that's reassuring. Anyhow, Melody, the dog walker, said she handed Avery the leash while they were behind the trailer. Then Melody walked away, leaving Avery alone."

Melody had given the police the perfect set up. She told them she handed the leash to Avery and then walked away, leaving Avery alone at the scene of the crime. I decided to let my own theory percolate a bit longer.

"Do they have anything else connecting Avery to the murder?" I asked.

Briggs shook his head as he nibbled a wing. He grabbed a napkin to wipe his mouth and fingers. "They've got motive and the bag and witnesses that saw her near the trailer, but it's a flimsy case at the moment. Burke said he interviewed a few people who know Avery well. They can all attest to the fact that she has a short fuse and terrible temper."

"I'll say." The affirmation slipped out before I could stop it. I peered up to see if Briggs had noticed. He had. Naturally.

"What do you mean? Did you have an encounter with Avery?"

"Yes, well no, it's just that—" I was sounding like a teenager trying to explain why I was out way past curfew. I straightened my posture and cleared my throat, giving me a chance to collect myself. "I told you I was at the dog show." I broke eye contact and fiddled with my napkin, a rookie mistake. "I saw Avery lose her temper when Ellen won the trophy. That's the only encounter, and it wasn't really an encounter but more of an observation."

Briggs sat silently across the table, letting me stew in my own dishonesty. He knew I was a terrible liar. I was even worse when I was sitting across from his thoughtful yet inquisitive detective face. And those dark brown eyes.

"What about the other encounter?" he asked.

I shrugged. "It wasn't a big deal."

"Ah ha, so there was another encounter. I knew it." He rewarded his cleverness with a drink of beer.

"You tricked me," I said. "I don't think I have to tell you anything since you used your detective dark arts to pry the confession out of me."

He laughed. "It was hardly dark arts. Let's just say, I know when Lacey Pinkerton, the world's worst liar, is, in fact, lying." He leaned back against his chair. "Why don't you tell me about the encounter."

I sighed. "Fine. But it was no big deal. I wasn't in any danger. Besides, my trusty bird with his menacing beak kept a watchful eye . . . " my voice trailed off as I realized my words were sending a shot of adrenaline through him.

The table wobbled as he sat forward. "What do you mean you weren't in danger and King was keeping an eye on you? Did Avery Hinkle attack you?" His jaw was doing the tiny twitch thing it did when he was upset.

"No, James, she didn't attack me. At least not physically. Thankfully. Avery Hinkle barged into the shop this evening when I was about to close up. She'd heard I was talking to her boyfriend and Vivian at the dog boutique. She asked in very unfriendly terms for me to stop."

"Explain very unfriendly terms, Lacey."

"There were a few baseless threats like 'you better stay out of my business' and things like that," I talked airily to let him know I wasn't the least bit scared of her intrusion, even though it definitely shook me up. "She is still convinced that Ellen gave her dog peanut butter before the show."

"Which shows she's still obsessing about it. I want you to stay clear of this case until they bring her in and press charges. You saw what she did to Ellen. She is obviously capable of cold-blooded murder. I'm not kidding, Lacey. You need to just drop this one and let the police handle it." He pulled out his phone.

"Who are you calling?" I asked.

"I'm calling Burke. I'm going to have him interview you so you can tell him the details of your encounter with Miss Hinkle." He held the phone and tried to swipe through his contact list with his left hand but wasn't having much luck. "Darn it. Why can't I figure out how to swipe with my useless left thumb?"

I reached over and patted his arm. "Wait, James. Put the phone down and hear me out. I haven't told you all the things *I've* found out about the murder. Yes, she has a terrible temper and motive and opportunity, but I don't think Avery Hinkle killed Ellen Joyner."

Briggs lowered his phone and looked up with a questioning brow. "No? Who do you think did it? The couple that lost the lawsuit seemed to have an airtight alibi."

"It wasn't the Cramptons. I think Melody Langley, the woman who"—I held up air quotes—"discovered the body, killed her. It was actually a fairly clever plan, look distressed and despondent and rightfully horrified about finding Ellen on the floor of her trailer with a bag over her head. It took any possible suspicion away from Melody. After all, how many times does the murderer actually pretend to find the victim?"

He moved his head side to side. "It happens occasionally. Especially when it's a murder within the same house. But go on. I want to hear why you think Melody killed Ellen."

"Not only did she kill Ellen but she also sabotaged the dog show. Melody is the one who gave Belvedere peanut butter. She knew Avery would throw a fit and a make a scene, which, in turn, would make her the logical suspect in Ellen's murder."

There were so many fragments to pull together to make a cohesive story, I sensed Briggs was getting more confused.

He shook his head. "Hold on. So Melody killed Ellen just to frame Avery?"

"Oh no, not just to frame Avery. She definitely wanted to kill Ellen. It was a two for one kind of thing. She got rid of Ellen, and at the same time, with any luck, she would ruin Avery's life by letting her take the rap for murder."

Briggs picked up his beer, then thought better of it, muttering something about keeping his head clear. His phone rang as he put the bottle down. He pulled it out. "It's Burke." He got up to answer it and walked away from the table.

I nibbled on a piece of chicken while I waited patiently for him to finish the phone call. I hoped there would be more about the case. I was feeling pretty solid about my ideas, but I was going on a lot of assumptions.

"Yeah, we'll be right there," Briggs said as he hung up. "Well, my little button-nosed Sherlock. You might just be onto something. That was Burke. He said Melody Langley just showed up in tears at the station claiming she had something important to confess. I told them we'll be right there. I want to talk to her myself. I'm hoping my unofficial partner will join me since she seems to know more about this case than anyone"

I hopped up and saluted him. "Button-nosed Sherlock, at your service."

CHAPTER 35

On the drive to the station, I worked to replay and organize all the interactions I'd had with Melody since I first met her at the dog show. I hoped that some of them would come in handy. But then, if she was already confessing the whole thing to the police, I wasn't going to be needed at all. That was sort of disappointing, but at least I could feel satisfaction in having solved the case before the confession. It just wasn't as exciting.

Briggs and I arrived at the Chesterton Precinct. It was quite a bit bigger than our quaint little Port Danby station.

"Detective Briggs," a man at the front desk said as we walked inside. "How is the arm? I heard you had a little run in with a bad guy and a knife."

"How are you doing, Officer Nettles?" Briggs lifted his arm. "Just glad it was a small knife and a clumsy bad guy. Is Burke around?"

"Yeah, he's in back." Officer Nettles, a middle aged man with a paunch and a kind grin, nodded politely at me.

"Nettles, I don't know if you've ever met Lacey." Briggs motioned toward me.

Nettles stood up and put out his hand. "We haven't met but I've heard all about that terrific nose of hers. Welcome to the Chesterton Precinct."

"Thank you and my nose thanks you for the nice compliment."

Nettles chuckled. "Why don't you two head back. I'll buzz you through."

We walked through the security gate and through the metal door leading to the various sections of the precinct. The first few rooms had windows, so we could see directly inside. In one room, Officer Burke and a woman officer were sitting across a table from Melody. Melody had a tissue bunched in her fingers. They had provided her with a bottle of water. She looked distraught and pale with worry.

"Darn," I whispered, even though I was sure the glass window and walls were too thick to hear through. "She's already confessed."

Briggs rubbed the short beard on his unshaven chin. "I don't think so. If she was confessing, they'd have her in an interrogation room with a one way mirror and security cameras. They use these rooms to talk to witnesses."

I looked at him. "I don't understand."

"Me neither." Rather than disrupt the room by entering, with my help, Briggs sent Burke a text that we were out in the hallway.

Burke stepped out just a minute later.

"What's going on?" Briggs asked. "I thought she came in to confess."

"That's what she said. Apparently, she didn't realize what the word *confess* means inside a police station. She came in to confess that she hadn't given us all the facts. She knew something about Avery Hinkle that she hadn't told us before. She said she was trying to protect a friend."

I snorted lightly. Both men looked at me. "I'm sorry but they are not friends. Avery is dating Melody's ex-fiancé, and she has not gotten over the breakup."

Briggs looked at Burke. "Were you aware of that?"

Burke sputtered and fidgeted with his belt for a second. "None of that ever came up in interviews with the two women."

Briggs shot me a quick wink.

"The details Miss Langley provided are pretty damning," Burke said. "She claims that she saw Miss Hinkle steal a purple collar off of a vendor's table just after the dog show. She also said that she wasn't telling the complete truth about her account of the interactions with Miss Hinkle behind the victim's trailer. After handing Miss Hinkle her dog, Miss Langley walked away, but when she looked back, she saw Miss Hinkle walking up the steps of the victim's trailer. She said at the time, she worried Miss Hinkle was going inside to confront Ellen Joyner about the sabotage. Miss Langley also said it looked as if Miss Hinkle might have been concealing something under her shirt."

I stopped a second snort. "I'm sorry but there would be no question about her concealing that thick plastic bag." I looked at Briggs for confirmation. "Miss Hinkle was wearing a very tight t-shirt, a few sizes too small, in fact." With her rude attack this afternoon, I found it quite easy to be catty about her too tight clothes.

Briggs nodded. "I do remember she was wearing a snug shirt. It wouldn't have been easy for her to conceal the bag."

The door to the witness room opened and the female officer stepped out. "Officer Burke," she said, and for the first time she realized the bearded man standing next to Burke was Detective Briggs. She flashed a pleasant smile. "Detective Briggs, I didn't recognize you with all the facial hair. It suits you," she added unnecessarily, along with another shiny white smile. She pulled her fascinated gaze from the bearded man and turned her attention back to Burke. "Miss Langley would like to go home. She is frightened about being here when they bring in Miss Hinkle. Should I let her go?"

"Not yet," Briggs answered first. "And don't send anyone out to pick up Miss Hinkle yet. There may be a problem with your witness. If she lost her fiancé to Miss Hinkle, then she might be compromised."

While he spoke, something else dawned on me. "Where was Pebbles?" the question spurted out loud before I could stop it.

All three officers looked at me.

"Pebbles," I repeated. "Melody, Miss Langley, was walking Ellen Joyner's poodle, Pebbles, around the dog show. She came up to the dog boutique vendor's table, that was the table with the dog collars. She asked if we had seen Ellen. Melody claimed Ellen had handed off Pebbles to her after the show because Ellen was suffering from a headache, a result of all the drama. She said Ellen didn't want to leave the dog unattended in a pen because Avery was so mad. She thought there might be some kind of retribution."

"I'd say that makes our case even stronger against Avery Hinkle," Burke said. "If the victim feared some kind of revenge—"

"Yes but if Melody's account was true, then she would still have had Pebbles when she said she handed off Belvedere to Avery. But neither Avery nor Melody mentioned that Pebbles was also with them behind the trailer. It was all a lie. Melody used Pebbles as a prop, pretending that she was looking for Ellen to hand her dog back. Ellen had never given her to Melody in the first place. She must have taken her from the pen and walked her around pretending to be looking for Ellen. But all along, Melody knew Ellen was dead because she had killed her."

An awkward silence followed. I couldn't tell if I had lost them with my convoluted theory or if they were just shocked that I knew so much about that day.

"But what motive would Melody have to kill Ellen? I understand she's not even a competitor. She's a professional dog groomer." Burke wasn't convinced, and he didn't seem altogether happy that I was swooping in to undermine his case. I supposed that was to be expected. I was almost hesitant about telling him the motive. I was certain he had no idea about the shampoo debacle.

Briggs was looking at me, waiting for a response, so I forged ahead.

"Melody had motive. Ellen Joyner was selling a very popular shampoo on her site. It's called Lavender Pooch." I looked at Briggs. "Remember she gave us a business card that night on the beach."

Briggs twisted his mouth a bit in embarrassment and both officers flashed teasing grins. "Yes, I remember," Briggs said quickly. "What does that have to do with Melody?"

"Melody and Ellen had been close friends at one point. Melody is the person who came up with the formula for Lavender Pooch. Ellen stole the idea and marketed it as her own. She was making a small fortune with the shampoo, but she never gave Melody credit or compensation."

Briggs looked at Officer Burke. "I'd like a few minutes with the witness."

"Absolutely," Burke said.

Briggs reached the door and motioned for me to follow. "You come too. You're the case expert." I scurried with excitement to follow him into the room.

Melody's eyes nearly bulged from her face when she saw me walk into the room. She forced a weak smile but didn't say a word.

Briggs nodded at her. "Miss Langley, I'm Detective Briggs. I believe we spoke at the park on the day of the murder. You know Miss Pinkerton."

"Yes." Her voice was thin and hoarse. She cleared her throat. "Yes, she helped me when I discovered poor Ellen on the floor of the trailer." Her voice trembled, but I wasn't convinced it was genuine. "I thought there was still something we could do to help her. That's why I ripped open the bag so she could breathe." She pressed her knuckles to her lips to stifle a sob. I reconsidered my theory for all of a second. The woman was a great actor.

Briggs seemed to come to the same conclusion. "Miss Langley, it is my duty to inform you that you may have an attorney present at any time."

Melody sat back as if the wind had been knocked out of her. "For what? I'm just a witness." Her voice waver was real this time, only it had nothing to do with grief. "I knew I should have left well enough alone. I was only trying to help."

"Miss Langley," Briggs said with that cool deep tone that I loved. "Would you like to call an attorney?"

She crossed her arms defiantly. "I have no reason for an attorney. My only crime was trying to help the police solve Ellen's murder."

"Then you waive your right," Briggs said and pulled out chairs for both of us. "I'll get right to it, Miss Langley. Is it true that Ellen Joyner was making a profit on a dog shampoo that you created?"

She was thrown way off by the first question. Her eyes flicked my direction and then back to Briggs. "Yes but I hardly see what that has to do with anything. It was a few years ago. I hardly think about it." She shrugged to punctuate her indifference.

"Let's move on then to the day of the murder. You discovered Ellen Joyner on the floor of her trailer at approximately four in the afternoon. What were you doing prior to that?"

She wriggled nervously on her chair. Her eyes flicked my direction again. She knew I had been there the entire afternoon and that I had seen her with Pebbles. "I was taking care of Ellen's dog, Pebbles. Ellen wasn't feeling well after Avery made the scene at the dog show. She asked me to look after Pebbles because she was afraid Avery might harm the dog." She pointed at me. "She was there. She was at the vendor tables when I was looking for Ellen." She looked to me for confirmation.

I nodded. "Yes, I saw you with Pebbles and heard you telling Vivian that you were looking for Ellen."

A tiny smile appeared. She looked confidently at Briggs. "There you have it. That's what I was doing. But then I needed to clean up my own trailer, so I decided to just put Pebbles back into her pen. That's when I decided to check Ellen's trailer again. That's when I found her. Then I rushed out for some help." She nodded at me. "You were there."

"Yes, yes I was."

"Yes, that all checks out, Miss Langley. Only one part of the story doesn't add up," Briggs said.

Her cheeks drained of color. "I don't understand."

"That day and during follow up interviews with both you and Miss Hinkle, you were walking her dog, Belvedere. You were behind Ellen's trailer walking the dog in a grassy area. That is where Miss Hinkle found you and took her dog back."

"That's right," she said with a chin thrust. "And I left right after, but as I told Officer Burke, when I glanced back Avery was climbing the steps of Ellen's trailer."

"Where was Pebbles?" he asked. It was a simple enough question, but her face contorted in every direction.

"I don't understand," she finally sputtered. I had never been in an interview like this before, but my guess was that our suspect was starting to crack.

"You said you were taking care of Pebbles for Ellen. She had a headache and asked you to watch the dog while she rested. Where was Pebbles while you were walking Belvedere?"

"Why, why she was right there too. It is possible to walk two dogs at once."

Briggs pulled out his notebook and glanced through his notes from that day. "Interesting, there was no mention of Pebbles in your interview. Miss Hinkle didn't mention it either." He pulled out his phone and dialed. "Yes, Officer Burke, could you call Avery

Hinkle and ask her if Ellen's dog, Pebbles, was standing with Miss Langley when she picked up Belvedere behind the trailer."

Melody was wriggling so much on her chair, I thought she might slip off.

Briggs put the phone away.

"Avery will just lie," she blurted somewhat hysterically. "She's a lying, backstabber. The kind of friend who will steal your boyfriend and then flaunt it for all the world to see. She's a horrid person. They all are. The entire dog show circuit." Tears were flowing now. She tapped her own chest. "I'm the one who makes the dogs show worthy. I make them beautiful and perfect, and what do I get? Stabbed in the back."

Briggs sat forward and cleared his throat. "Miss Langley, I'll ask you again, would you like to have an attorney present?"

She crumpled back against the chair. "Yes," she said weakly. "Yes, I would."

CHAPTER 36

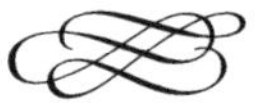

I hummed an old Rolling Stones' tune as I finished potting some basil plants.

"Someone is in a good mood," Ryder said as he finished arranging a dozen roses. "Guess that's the happy hum of someone who solved a murder."

"It sure is." I rinsed my hands. I was feeling pretty pleased with myself. The police were about to haul Avery Hinkle in for murder, based on false evidence presented by the real killer. (Not that I would have minded if Avery Hinkle had suffered a false arrest for a few hours after her last visit to my shop.) Once Melody's shell cracked and her story started falling apart, she poured her heart out, trying to frame herself as the victim. Avery had stolen her fiancé and Ellen stole her shampoo formula. It was easy to see why she would be angry, but most people in those types of situations didn't resort to murder. She knew both women well enough to plot her murder and frame up in advance of the show. Melody knew Avery would throw a fit if she thought Ellen stole the trophy from her. And Avery reacted just the way Melody predicted. She then killed Ellen, knowing everyone saw Avery's tantrum. It made her the logical suspect. She'd even planned out what to tell the police the first time to make it look as if she was protecting Avery. Then came Melody's dramatic show at the police station where she added in more incriminating but fake details because the *guilt* of not telling the truth had gotten to her. It was a fairly impressive murder plan, but she forgot about Pebbles.

I walked over to where Ryder was finishing up his bouquet. "I guess Lola is probably humming happily too," I said, "now that her mom is back in Europe."

Ryder didn't answer at first. He put down the ribbon he was holding and pulled out his phone. "You can't tell Lola I have this or that I showed it to you, but, well—there was such a scene at the airport, people were filming it. So I decided to join them."

He showed me the screen on his phone and hit play. Lola and her mom were hugging and crying and creating a goodbye scene worthy of an Oscar winning movie.

"Oh my gosh, that is a lot of crying and hugging," I said. "Are you sure that red hair and Beatles t-shirt belong to Lola?"

Ryder laughed and put the phone away. "Oh, it was our Lo-lo all right. The phony. She complained about her mom the whole time but when it was time to say goodbye those two acted as if they were parting forever."

I smiled. "I'm sort of glad it went like that. Aren't you?"

He nodded. "Yeah, it was kind of cool. Only I don't dare bring it up because that sends Lola into a tizzy. So lips sealed."

I pulled the zipper across. "You can count on me." The door opened. I was pleasantly surprised to see a handsome detective with an even heavier and darker beard.

I rubbed my chin between my finger and thumb. "I'm trying to decide if you should keep the beard. It makes you look a little more mysterious."

Briggs reached up and scratched under his chin. "It also makes me feel itchy so don't spend too much time deciding. It goes as soon as the bandage comes off my right arm. Hey, Ryder, how's it going?"

"Great. I heard my boss solved a murder case," Ryder boasted.

Briggs' brown eyes were smiling at me. "That she did. And I've come to take her to lunch as a reward."

"And because you are bored out of your mind," I added.

"That too." He took my hand. "Let's go button-nosed Sherlock. You can fill me in on just how you solved a case long before the police. Maybe I'll learn something."

VEGAN TRAIL MIX COOKIES

View recipe online at londonlovett.com/recipe-box

Vegan Trail Mix
COOKIES

Ingredients:

1 1/2 cups rolled oats - separated
 -1 cup of oats processed into flour
 -1/2 cup of oats left whole
1/2 cup almonds, processed into flour
1/2 tsp baking soda
1/2 tsp baking powder
1/2 tsp salt
1 1/2 tsp vanilla
1 flax egg (1 Tbsp ground flax seed combined with 3 Tbsp water)
3 oz vegan butter, softened
1 Tbsp maple syrup
1/4 cup almond butter (can substitute peanut or other nut butter)
3/4 cup organic brown sugar
2 Tbsp sunflower seeds
1/4 cup dried cranberries
1/4 cup chocolate chips

Directions:

1. Pre-heat oven to 325°. In a small bowl, mix together 1 Tbsp ground flax and 3 Tbsp water and set aside to make your flax egg.

2. In a blender or food processor turn 1 cup of the oats into flour. Process the almonds into a flour the same way. (Be careful not to over blend/process the almonds or you'll end up with almond butter.)

3. In a large bowl, combine the oat flour, almond flour, baking soda, baking powder, salt and whole oats.

4. In a medium bowl, mix together the softened vegan butter, almond butter, brown sugar, maple syrup, flax egg and vanilla until well combined.

5. Add the wet ingredients to the large dry bowl and stir to combine. Mix in the sunflower seeds, cranberries and chocolate chips. You can get creative here and add other mix-ins such as chopped nuts and shredded coconut if you'd like.

6. Using a cookie scoop (mine is 2 Tbsp) or a spoon, scoop cookies onto a baking sheet and press lightly to flatten. Recipe makes 18-22 cookies.

7. Bake at 325° for 12-15 minutes, until dry on top.

8. Allow cookies to cool for a few minutes before transferring to a cooling rack.

9. ENJOY!

There will be more from Port Danby soon. In the meantime, check out my new Starfire Cozy Mystery series! Books 1 & 2 are now available.

Los Angeles, 1923. The land of movie stars and perpetual sunshine has a stylish new force to be reckoned with—**Poppy Starfire,** *Private Investigator.*

See all available titles: LondonLovett.com

ABOUT THE AUTHOR

London Lovett is the author of the Port Danby, Starfire and Firefly Junction Cozy Mystery series. She loves getting caught up in a good mystery and baking delicious, new treats!

Join London Lovett's Secret Sleuths!:
facebook.com/groups/londonlovettssecretsleuths/

Subscribe to London's newsletter at www.londonlovett.com to never miss an update.

London loves to hear from readers. Feel free to reach out to her on Facebook: Facebook.com/londonlovettwrites, Follow on Instagram: @londonlovettwrites, Or send a quick email to londonlovettwrites@gmail.com.

Made in the USA
Middletown, DE
16 July 2019